Large Print Sel
Sellers, Alexandra.
Sheikh's woman

SHEIKH'S WOMAN

Alexandra Sellers

First published in Great Britain 2001 as part of 100% Male Large Print edition 2004 Silhouette Books Limited, Eton House, 18-24 Paradise Road, Richmond, Surrey TW9 1SR

ISBN 0 373 04924 2

Set in Times Roman 16½ on 18 pt.
36-0804-45873

Printed and bound in Great Britain
by Antony Rowe Ltd, Chippenham, Wiltshire

ALEXANDRA SELLERS

is the author of over twenty-five novels and a feline language text published in 1997 and still selling.

Born and raised in Canada, Alexandra first came to London as a drama student. Now she lives near Hampstead Heath with her husband, Nick. They share housekeeping with Monsieur, who came in through the window one day and announced, as cats do, that he was staying.

What she would miss most on a desert island is shared laughter.

Readers can write to Alexandra at PO Box 9449, London NW3 2WH.

For my sister Joy,
who held it all together
in the bad times and makes things
even better in the good.

Prologue

She crouched in the darkness, whimpering as the pain gripped her. He had made her wait too long. She had warned him, but he'd pretended not to believe her ''lies.'' And now, in an empty, dirty alley, nowhere to go, no time to get there, her time was upon her.

Pain stabbed her again, and she cried out involuntarily. She pressed a hand over her mouth and looked behind her down the alley. Of course by now he had discovered her flight. He was already after her. If he had heard that cry…

She staggered to her feet again, picked up

the bag, began a shuffling run. Her heart was beating so hard! The drumming in her head seemed to drown out thought. She ran a few paces and then doubled over again as the pain came. Oh, Lord, not here! Please, please, not in an alley, like an animal, to be found when she was most helpless, when the baby would be at his mercy.

He would have no mercy. The pain ebbed and she ran on, weeping, praying. *"Ya Allah!"* Forgive me, protect me.

Suddenly, as if in answer, she sensed a deeper darkness in the shadows. She turned towards it without questioning, and found herself in a narrower passage. The darkness was more intense here, and she stared blindly until her eyes grew accustomed.

There was a row of garages on either side of a short strip of paving. Then she saw what had drawn her, what her subconscious mind— or her guardian angel—had already seen: one door was ajar. She bit her lip. Was there someone inside, a fugitive like herself? But another clutch of pain almost knocked her to her knees. As she bent double, stifling her cry, she heard a shout. A long way distant, but she feared what was behind her more than what might be ahead.

Sobbing with mingled pain and terror, she stumbled towards the open door and pushed her way inside.

One

——

"Can you hear me? Anna, can you hear my voice?"

It was like being dragged through long, empty rooms. Anna groaned protestingly. What did they want from her? Why didn't they let her sleep?

"Move your hand if you can hear my voice, Anna. Can you move your hand?"

It took huge effort, as if she had to fight through thick syrup.

"That's excellent! Now, can you open your eyes?"

Abruptly something heavy seemed to smash

down inside her skull, driving pain through every cell. She moaned.

"I'm afraid you're going to have a pretty bad headache," said the voice, remorselessly cheerful, determinedly invasive. "Come now, Anna! Open your eyes!"

She opened her eyes. The light was too bright. It hurt. A woman in a navy shirt with white piping was gazing at her. "Good, there you are!" she said, in a brisk Scots accent. "What's your name?"

"Anna," said Anna. "Anna Lamb."

The woman nodded. "Good, Anna."

"What happened? Where am I?" Anna whispered. She was lying in a grey cubicle on a narrow hospital trolley, fully dressed except for shoes. "Why am I in hospital?" The hammer slammed down again. "My head!"

"You've been in an accident, but you're going to be fine. Just a wee bit concussed. Your baby's fine."

Your baby. A different kind of pain smote her then, and she lay motionless as cold enveloped her heart.

"My baby died," she said, her voice flat as

the old, familiar lifelessness seeped through
her.

The nurse was taking Anna's blood pressure, but at this she looked up. ''She's absolutely fine! The doctor's just checking her over
now,'' she said firmly. ''I don't know why you
wanted to give birth in a taxicab, but it seems
you made a very neat job of it.''

She leaned forward and pulled back one of
Anna's eyelids, shone light from a tiny flash-
light into her eye.

''In a taxicab?'' Anna repeated. ''But—''

Confused memories seemed to pulsate in her
head, just out of reach.

''You're a very lucky girl!'' said the cheerful nurse, moving down to press her abdomen
with searching fingers. She paused, frowning,
and pressed again.

Anna was silent, her eyes squeezed tight,
trying to think through the pain and confusion
in her head. Meanwhile the nurse poked and
prodded, frowned a little, made notes, poked
again. ''Lift up, please?'' she murmured, and
with competent hands carried on the exami-
nation.

When it was over, she stood looking down at Anna, sliding her pen into the pocket of her uniform trousers. A little frown had gathered between her eyebrows.

"Do you remember giving birth, Anna?"

Pain rushed in at her. The room suddenly filling with people, all huddled around her precious newborn baby, while she cried, "Let me see him, why can't I hold him?" and then...*Anna, I'm sorry, I'm so very sorry. We couldn't save your baby.*

"Yes," she said lifelessly, gazing at the nurse with dry, stretched eyes, her heart a lump of stone. "I remember."

A male head came around the cubicle's curtain. "Staff, can you come, please?"

The Staff Nurse gathered up her instruments. "Maternity Sister will be down as soon as she can get away, but it may be a while, Anna. They've got staff shortages there, too, tonight, and a Caes—"

A light tap against the partition wall preceded the entrance of a young nurse, looking desperately tired but smiling as she rolled a wheeled bassinet into the room.

"Oh, nurse, there you are! How's the bairn?'' said the Staff Nurse, sounding not altogether pleased.

The bairn was crying with frustrated fury, and neither of the nurses heard the gasp that choked Anna. A storm of emotion seemed to seize her as she lifted herself on her elbows and, ignoring the punishment this provoked from the person in her head who was beating her nerve endings, struggled to sit up.

"Baby?" Anna cried. "Is that *my baby?*"

Meanwhile, the young nurse wheeled the baby up beside the trolley, assuring Anna, "Yes, she is. A lovely little girl." Anna looked into the bassinet, closed her eyes, looked again.

The baby stopped crying suddenly. She was well wrapped up in hospital linen, huge eyes open, silent now but frowning questioningly at the world.

"Oh, dear God!" Anna exclaimed, choking on the emotion that surged up inside. "Oh, my baby! Was it just a nightmare, then? Oh, my darling!"

"It's not unusual for things to get mixed up

after a bang on the head like yours, but everything will sort itself out,'' said the Staff Nurse. ''We'll keep you in for observation for a day or two, but there's nothing to worry about.''

Anna hardly heard. ''I want to hold her!'' she whispered, convulsively reaching towards the bassinet. The young nurse obligingly picked the baby up and bent over Anna. Her hungry arms wrapping the infant, Anna sank back against the pillows.

Her heart trembled with a joy so fierce it hurt, obliterating for a few moments even the pain in her head. She drew the little bundle tight against her breast, and gazed hungrily into the flower face.

She was beautiful. Huge questioning eyes, dark hair that lay on her forehead in feathery curls, wide, full mouth which was suddenly, adorably, stretched by a yawn.

All around one eye there was a mocha-hued shadow that added an inexplicably piquant charm to her face. She gazed at Anna, serenely curious.

''She looks like a bud that's just opened,'' Anna marvelled. ''She's so fresh, so new!''

"She's lovely," agreed the junior nurse, while the Staff Nurse hooked the clipboard of Anna's medical notes onto the foot of the bed.

"Good, then," she said, nodding. "Now you'll be all right here till Maternity Sister comes. Nurse, I'll see you for a moment, please."

The sense of unreality returned when she was left alone with the baby. Anna gazed down into the sweet face from behind a cloud of pain and confusion. She couldn't seem to think.

The baby fell asleep, just like that. Anna bent to examine her. The birthmark on her eye was very clear now that the baby's eyes were closed. Delicate, dark, a soft smudging all around the eye. Anna was moved by it. She supposed such a mark could be considered a blemish, but somehow it managed to be just the opposite.

"You'll set the fashion, my darling," Anna whispered with a smile, cuddling the baby closer. "All the girls will be painting their eyes with makeup like that in the hopes of making themselves as beautiful as you."

It made the little face even more vulnerable, drew her, touched her heart. She couldn't remember ever having seen such a mark before. Was this kind of thing inherited? No one in her family had anything like it.

Was it a dream, that memory of another child? Tiny, perfect, a beautiful, beautiful son…but so white. They had allowed her to hold him, just for a few moments, to say goodbye. Her heart had died then. She had felt it go cold, turn to ice and then stone. They had encouraged her to weep, but she did not weep. Grief required a heart.

Was that a dream?

She was terribly tired. She bent to lay the sleeping infant back in the bassinet. Then she leaned down over the tiny, fragile body, searching her face for clues.

"Who is your father?" she whispered. "Where am I? What's happening to me?"

Her head ached violently. She lay back against the pillows and wished the lights weren't so bright.

*   *   *

*"My daughter, you must prepare yourself
for some excellent news."*

*She smiled trustingly at her mother. "Is it
the embassy from the prince?" she asked, for
the exciting information had of course seeped
into the harem.*

*"The prince's emissaries and I have dis-
cussed the matter of your marriage with the
prince. Now I have spoken with your father,
whose care is all for you. Such a union will
please him very much, my daughter, for he desires peace with the prince and his people."*

*She bowed. "I am happy to be the means of
pleasing my father…. And the prince? What
manner of man do they say he is?"*

*"Ah, my daughter, he is a young man to
please any woman. Handsome, strong, capable
in all the manly arts. He has distinguished
himself in battle, too, and stories are told of
his bravery."*

*She sighed her happiness. "Oh, mother, I
feel I love him already!" she said.*

Anna awoke, not knowing what had dis-
turbed her. A tall, dark man was standing at

the foot of her trolley, reading her chart. There was something about him… She frowned, trying to concentrate. But sleep dragged her eyes shut.

"They're both fine," she heard when she opened them next, not sure whether it was seconds or minutes later. The man was talking to a young woman who looked familiar. After a second Anna's jumbled brain recognized the junior nurse.

The man drew her eyes. He was strongly charismatic. Handsome as a pirate captain, exotically dark and obviously foreign. Masculine, strong, handsome—and impossibly clean for London, as if he had come straight from a massage and shave at his club without moving through the dust and dirt of city traffic.

He was wearing a grey silk lounge suit which looked impeccably Savile Row. A round diamond glowed with dark fire from a heavy, square gold setting on his ring finger. Heavy cuff links on the French cuffs of his cream silk shirt matched it. On his other hand she saw the flash of an emerald.

He didn't look at all overdressed or showy.

It sat on him naturally. He was like an aristo-
crat in a period film. Dreamily she imagined
him in heavy brocade, with a fall of lace at
wrist and throat.

She blinked, coming drowsily more awake.
The junior nurse was glowing, as if the man's
male energy had stirred and ignited something
in her, in spite of her exhaustion. She was mes-
merized.

"Because he's mesmerizing," Anna muttered.

Suddenly recalled to her duties, the nurse
glanced at her patient. "You're awake!" she
murmured.

The man turned and looked at her, too, his
eyes dark and his gaze piercing. Anna blinked.
There was a mark on his eye just like her
baby's. A dark irregular smudge that enhanced
both his resemblance to a pirate and his exotic
maleness.

"Anna!" he exclaimed. A slight accent
furred his words attractively. "Thank God you
and the baby were not hurt! What on earth
happened?"

She felt very, very stupid. "Are you the doctor?" she stammered.

His dark eyes snapped into an expression of even greater concern, and he made a sound that was half laughter, half worry. He bent down and clasped her hand. She felt his fingers tighten on her, in unmistakable silent warning.

"Darling!" he exclaimed. "The nurse says you don't remember the accident, but I hope you have not forgotten your own husband!"

Two
—

Husband? Anna stared. Her mouth opened. "I'm not—" she began. He pressed her hand again, and she broke off. Was he really her husband? How could she be married and not remember? Her heart kicked. Had a man like him fallen in love with her, chosen her?

"Are we married?" she asked.

He laughed again, with a thread of warning in his tone that she was at a loss to figure. "Look at our baby! Does she not tell you the truth?"

The birthmark was unmistakable. But how could such a thing be? "I can't remember things,'' she told him in a voice which trembled, trying to hold down the panic that suddenly swept her. ''I can't remember anything.''

A husband—how could she have forgotten? Why? She squeezed her eyes shut, and stared into the inner blackness. She knew who she was, but everything else eluded her.

She opened her eyes. He was smiling down at her in deep concern. He was so *attractive!* The air around him seemed to crackle with vitality. Suddenly she *wanted* it to be true. She wanted him to be her husband, wanted the right to lean on him. She felt so weak, and he looked so strong. He looked like a man used to handling things.

Someone was screaming somewhere. *''Nurse, nurse!''* It was a hoarse, harsh cry. She put her hand to her pounding head. ''It's so noisy,'' she whispered.

''We'll soon have her somewhere quieter,'' said the junior nurse, hastily reassuring. ''I'll just go and check with Maternity again.'' She slipped away, leaving Anna alone with the baby and the man who was her husband.

"Come, I want to get you out of here," he said.

There was something odd about his tone. She tried to focus, but her head ached desperately, and she seemed to be behind a thick curtain separating her from the world.

"But where?" she asked weakly. "This is a hospital."

"You are booked into a private hospital. They are waiting to admit you. It is far more pleasant there—they are not short-staffed and overworked. I want a specialist to see and reassure you."

He had already drawn Anna's shoes from under the bed. Anna, her head pounding, obediently sat up on the edge of the trolley bed and slipped her feet into them. Meanwhile, he neatly removed the pages from the clipboard at the foot of her bed, folded and slipped them into his jacket pocket.

"Why are you taking those?" she asked stupidly.

He flicked her an inscrutable look, then picked up the baby with atypical male confidence. "Where is your bag, Anna? Did you have a bag?"

"Oh—!" She put her hand to her forehead, remembering the case she had packed so carefully…and then had carried out of the hospital when it was all over. That long, slow walk with empty arms. Her death march.

"My bag," she muttered, but her brain would not engage with the problem, with the contradiction.

"Never mind, we can get it later." He pulled aside the curtain of the cubicle, glanced out, and then turned to her. "Come!"

Her head ached with ten times the ferocity as she obediently stood. He wrapped his free arm around her back and drew her out of the cubicle, and she instinctively obeyed his masculine authority.

The casualty ward was like an overcrowded bad dream. They passed a young man lying on a trolley, his face smashed and bloody. Another trolley held an old woman, white as her hair, her veins showing blue, eyes wild with fear. She was muttering something incomprehensible and stared at Anna with helpless fixity as they passed. Somewhere someone was half moaning, half screaming. That other voice still called for a nurse. A child's cry, high and broken, betrayed mingled pain and panic.

''My God, do you think it's like this all the time?'' Anna murmured.

''It is Friday night.''

They walked through the waiting room, where every seat was filled, and a moment later stepped out into the autumn night. Rain was falling, but softly, and she found the cold air a relief.

''Oh, that's better!'' Anna exclaimed, shivering a little in her thin shirt.

A long black limousine parked a few yards away purred into life and eased up beside them. Her husband opened the back door for her.

Anna drew back suddenly, without knowing why. ''What about my coat? Don't I have a coat?''

''The car is warm. Come, get in. You are tired.''

His voice soothed her fears, and the combination of obvious wealth and his commanding air calmed her. If he was her husband, she must be safe.

In addition to everything else, being upright was making her queasy. Anna gave in and slipped inside the luxurious passenger compartment, sinking gratefully down onto deep, superbly comfortable upholstery. He locked and shut the door.

She leaned back and her eyes closed. He spoke to the driver in a foreign language through the window, and a moment later the other passenger door opened, and her husband got inside with the baby. The limo began rolling forward immediately. Absently she clocked the driver picking up a mobile phone.

''Are we leaving, just like that? Don't I have to be signed out by a doctor or something?''

He shrugged. ''Believe me, the medical staff are terminally overworked here. When they discover the empty cubicle, the Casualty staff will assume you have been moved to a ward.''

Her head ached too much.

The darkness of the car was relieved at intervals by the filtered glow of passing lights. She watched him for a moment in light and shadow, light and shadow, as he settled the baby more comfortably.

''What's your name?'' she asked abruptly.

''I am Ishaq Ahmadi.''

''That doesn't even ring a faint bell!'' Anna exclaimed. ''Oh, my head! Do you—how long have we been married?''

There was a disturbing flick of his black gaze in darkness. It was as if he touched her, and a little electric shock was the result.

''There is no need to go on with this now, Anna,'' he said.

She jumped. ''What? What do you mean?''

His gaze remained compellingly on her.

''I remember my—who I *am*,'' she babbled, oddly made to feel guilty by his silent judgement, ''but I can't really remember my *life*. I *certainly* don't remember you. Or—or the baby, or anything. How long have we been married?''

He smiled and shrugged. ''Shall we say, two years?''

''Two years!'' She recoiled in horror.

''What of your life do you remember? Your mind is obviously not a complete blank. You must have something in there…you remember giving birth?''

''Yes, but…but what I remember is that my baby died.''

''Ah,'' he breathed, so softly she wasn't even sure she had heard it.

''They told me just now that wasn't true, but…'' She reached out to touch the baby in his arms. ''Oh, she's so sweet! Isn't she perfect? But I remember…'' Her eyes clenched against the spasm of pain. ''I *remember* holding my baby after he died.''

Her eyes searched his desperately in the darkness. ''Maybe that was a long time ago?'' she whispered.

''How long ago does it seem to you?''

The question seemed to trigger activity in her head. ''Six weeks, I think….''

You're going to have six wonderful weeks, Anna.

''Oh!'' she exclaimed, as a large piece of her life suddenly fell into place. ''I just remembered— I was on my way to a job in France. And Lisbet and Cecile were going to take me out for a really lovely dinner. It seems

to me I'm..." She squeezed her eyes shut.
"Aren't I supposed to be leaving on the Paris
train tomorrow...Saturday? Alan Mitching's
house in France." She opened her eyes. "Are
you saying that was more than two years in
the past?"

"What sort of a job?"

"He has a seventeenth-century place in the
Dordogne area...they want murals in the dining room. They want—wanted a Greek temple
effect. I've designed—" She broke off and
gazed at him in the darkness while the limousine purred through the wet, empty streets.
Traffic was light; it must be two or three in
the morning.

"I can remember making the designs, but I
can't remember doing the actual work." Panic
rose up in her. "Why can't I remember?"

"This state is not permanent. You will remember everything in time."

The baby stirred and murmured and she
watched as he shifted her a little.

"Let me hold her," she said hungrily.

For a second he looked as if he was going
to refuse, but she held out her arms, and he

slipped the tiny bundle into her embrace. A smile seemed to start deep within her and flow outwards all through her body and spirit to reach her lips. Her arms tightened. Oh, how lovely to have a living baby to hold against her heart in place of that horrible, hurting memory!

"Oh, you're so beautiful!" she whispered. She shifted her gaze to Ishaq Ahmadi. He was watching her. "Isn't she beautiful?"

A muscle seemed to tense in his jaw. "Yes," he said.

The chauffeur spoke through an intercom, and as her husband replied, Anna silently watched fleeting expressions wander over the baby's face, felt the perfection of the little body against her breast. Time seemed to disappear in the now. She lost the urgency of wanting to know how she had got to this moment, and was happy just to be in it.

When he spoke to her again, she came to with a little start and realized she had been almost asleep. "Can you remember how you came to be in the taxi with the baby?"

Nothing. Not even vague shadows. She shook her head. "No."

Then there was no sound except for rain and the flick of tires on the wet road. Anna was lost in contemplation again. She stroked the tiny fist. "Have we chosen a name for her?"

A passing headlight highlighted one side of his face, the side with the pirate patch over his eye.

"Her name is Safiyah."

"Sophia?"

"Yes, it is a name that will not seem strange to English ears. Safi is not so far from Sophy."

"Did we know it was going to be a girl?" she whispered, coughing as feeling closed her throat.

He glanced at her, the sleeping baby nestled so trustingly against her. "You are almost asleep," he said. "Let me take her."

He leaned over to lift the child from her arms. He was gentle and tender with her, but at the same time firm and confident, making Anna feel how safe the baby was with him.

Jonathan. "Oh!" she whispered.

"What is it?" Ishaq Ahmadi said, in a voice

of quiet command. "What have you remembered?"

"Oh, just when you took the baby from me...I..." She pressed her hands to her eyes. Not when he took the baby, but the sight of him holding the infant as if he loved her and was prepared to protect and defend the innocent.

"Tell me!"

She lifted her head to see him watching her with a look of such intensity she gasped. Suddenly she wondered how much of her past she had confided to her husband. Was he a tolerant man? Or had he wanted her to lie about her life before him?

She stammered, "Did—did—?" She swallowed, her mouth suddenly dry. "Did I tell you about...Jonathan? Jonathan Ryder?"

But even before the words were out she knew the answer was no.

Three

———

"**T**ell me now," Ishaq Ahmadi commanded softly.

She wanted to lean against him, wanted to feel his arm around her, protecting her, holding her. She must have that right, she told herself, but somehow she lacked the courage to ask him to hold her.

She had always wanted to pat the tigers at the zoo, too. Now it seemed as if she had finally found her very own personal tiger...but she had forgotten how she'd tamed him. And until she remembered that, something told her it would be wise to treat him with caution.

"Tell me about Jonathan Ryder."

Nervously she clasped her hands together, and suddenly a detail that had been nagging at her in the distance leapt into awareness.

"Why aren't I wearing a wedding ring?" she demanded, holding both hands spread out before her and staring at them. On her fingers were several silver rings of varied design. But none was a wedding band.

There was a long, pregnant pause. Through the glass panel separating them from the driver, she heard a phone ring. The driver answered and spoke into it, giving instructions, it seemed.

Still he only looked at her.

"Did I...have we split up?"

"No."

Just the bare syllable. His jaw seemed to tense, and she thought he threw her a look almost of contempt.

"About Jonathan," he prompted again.

If they were having trouble in the marriage, was it because he was jealous? Or because she had not told him things, shared her troubles?

She thought, *If I never told him about Jonathan, I should have.*

"Jonathan—Jonathan and I were going together for about a year. We were talking about moving in together, but it wasn't going to be simple, because we both owned a flat, and…well, it was taking us time to decide whether to sell his, or mine, or sell both and find somewhere new."

Her heart began to beat with anxiety. "It is really more than two years ago?"

"How long does it seem to you?"

"It feels as if we split up about six months ago. And then…"

"Why did you split up?"

"Because…did I not tell you any of this?"

"Tell me again," he repeated softly. "Perhaps the recital will help your memory recover."

She wanted to tell him. She wanted to share it with him, to make him her soul mate. Surely she must have told him, and he had understood? She couldn't have married a man who didn't understand, whom she couldn't share her deepest feelings with?

"I got pregnant unexpectedly." She looked at him and remembered that, sophisticated as he looked, he was from a different culture. "Does that shock you?"

"I am sure that birth control methods fail every day," he said.

That was not what she meant, but she lacked the courage to be more explicit.

"Having kids wasn't part of deciding to live together or anything, but once it happened I just—knew it was what I wanted. It was crazy, but it made me so happy! Jonathan didn't see it that way. He didn't want..."

Her head drooped, and the sound of suddenly increasing rain against the windows filled the gap.

"Didn't want the child?"

"He wanted me to have an abortion. He said we weren't ready yet. His career hadn't got off the ground, neither had mine. He—oh, he had a hundred reasons why it would be right one day but wasn't now. In a lot of ways he was right. But..." Anna shrugged. "I couldn't do it. We argued and argued. I understood him, but he never understood me. Never tried to. I kept saying, there's more to it than you want to believe. He wouldn't listen.''

''And did he convince you?''

''He booked an appointment for me, drove me down to the women's clinic…. On the way, he stopped the car at a red light, and—I got out,'' she murmured, staring at nothing. ''And just kept walking. I didn't look back, and Jonathan didn't come after me. He never called again. Well, once,'' she amended. ''A couple of months later he phoned to ask if I planned to name him as the father on the birth certificate.''

She paused, but Ishaq Ahmadi simply waited for her to continue. ''He said…he said he had no intention of being saddled with child support for the next twenty years. He had a job offer from Australia, and he was trying to decide whether to accept or not. And that was one of the criteria. If I was going to put his name down, he'd go to Australia.''

His hair glinted in the beam of a streetlight. They were on a highway. ''And what did you say?''

She shook her head. ''I hung up. We've never spoken since.''

''Did he go to Australia?''

''I never found out. I didn't want to know.'' She amended that. ''Didn't care.'' She glanced out the window.

''Where are we going?'' she asked. ''Where is the hospital?''

''North of London, in the country. Tell me what happened then.''

Her eyes burned. ''My friends were really, really great about it—do you know Cecile and Lisbet?''

''How could your husband not know your friends?''

''Are Cecile and Philip married?''

He gazed at her. ''Tell me about the baby, Anna.''

There was something in his attitude that made her uncomfortable. She murmured, ''I'm sorry if you didn't know before this. But maybe if you didn't, you should have. ''

''Undoubtedly.''

''*Did* you know?''

He paused. ''No.''

Anna bit her lip. She wondered if it was perhaps because she hadn't told him that she had reverted to this memory tonight. Had it weighed on her throughout the new pregnancy? Had fears for her new baby surfaced and found no outlet?

"Everything was fine. I was pretty stressed in some ways, but I didn't really have doubts about what I was doing. At the very end something went wrong. I was in labour for hours and hours, and then it was too late for a Caesarean...they used the Ventouse cap."

She swallowed, and her voice was suddenly expressionless. "It caused a brain haemorrhage. My baby died. They let me hold him, and he was...but there was a terrible bruise on his head...as if he was wearing a purple cap."

No tears came to moisten the heat of her eyes or ease the pain in her heart. Her perfect baby, paper white and too still, but looking as if he was thinking very hard and would open his eyes any moment...

She wondered if that was how she had ended up giving birth in the back of a cab.

Perhaps it was fear of a repetition that had made her leave it too late to get to the hospital.

"Why weren't you there?" she asked, surfacing from her thoughts to look at him. "Why didn't you take me to the hospital?"

"I flew in from abroad this evening. And this was six weeks ago?"

"That's how it feels to me. I feel as though it's the weekend I'm supposed to be going on that job to France, and that was about six weeks after the baby died. How long ago is that, really?"

"Did you ever feel, Anna, that you would like to—adopt a child? A baby to fill the void created by the death of your own baby?"

"It wouldn't have done me any good if I had. Why are you asking me these questions now? Didn't we—"

"Did you think of it—applying for adoption? Trying to find a baby?"

"No." She shook her head. "Sometimes in the street, you know, you pass a woman with a baby, or even a woman who's pregnant, and you just want to scream *It's not fair,* but—no, I just...I got pretty depressed, I wasn't doing much of anything till Lisbet conjured up this actor friend who wanted a mural in his place in France.''

She leaned over to caress the baby with a tender hand, then bent to kiss the perfectly formed little head. ''Oh, you are so beautiful!'' she whispered. She looked up, smiling. ''I hope I remember soon. I can't bear not knowing everything about her!''

He started to speak, and just then the car drew to a stop. Heavy rain was now thundering down on the roof, and all she could see were streaks of light from tall spotlights in the distance, as if they had entered some compound.

''Are we here?''

''Yes,'' he said, as the door beside her opened. The dark-skinned chauffeur stood in the rain with a large black umbrella, and Anna quickly slipped out onto a pavement that was leaping with water. She heard the swooping crack of another umbrella behind her. Then she was being ushered up a curiously narrow flight of steps and through a doorway.

She glanced around her as Ishaq, with the baby, came in the door behind her.

It was very curious for a hospital reception. A low-ceilinged room, softly lighted, lushly decorated in natural wood and rich tapestries. A row of matching little curtains seemed to be covering several small windows at intervals along the wall. There was a bar at one end, by a small dining table with chairs. In front of her she saw a cluster of plush armchairs around a coffee table. Anna frowned, trying to piece together a coherent interpretation of the scene, but her mind was very slow to function. She could almost hear her own wheels grinding.

A woman in an Eastern outfit that didn't look at all like a medical uniform appeared in the doorway behind the bar and came towards them. She spoke something in a foreign language, smiling and gesturing towards the sofa cluster. She moved to the entrance door behind them, dragged it fully shut and turned a handle. Still the pieces refused to fall into place.

Anna obediently sank down into an armchair. A second woman appeared. Dressed in another softly flowing outfit, with warm brown eyes and a very demure smile, she nodded and then descended upon the baby in Ishaq Ah-

madi's arms. She laughed and admired and
then exchanged a few sentences of question
and answer with Ishaq before taking the infant
in her own arms and, with another smile all
around, disappeared whence she had come.

"What's going on?" Anna demanded, as
alarm began to shrill behind the drowsy numb-
ness in her head.

"Your bed is ready," Ishaq murmured,
bending over her and slipping his hands
against her hips. At the touch of his strong
hands she involuntarily smiled. "In a few
minutes you can lie down and get some
sleep."

His hands lifted and she blinked stupidly
while he drew two straps up and snapped them
together over her hips. Under her feet she felt
the throb of engines, and at last the pieces fell
together.

"This isn't a hospital, this is a plane!" Anna
cried wildly.

Four

—

"Let me out," Anna said, her hands snapping to the seat belt.

Ishaq Ahmadi fastened his own seat belt and moved one casual hand to still hers as she struggled with the mechanism. "We have been cleared for immediate takeoff," he said.

"Stop the plane and let me off. Tell them to turn back," she cried, pushing at his hand, which was no longer casual. "Where are you taking us? I want my baby!"

"The woman you saw is a children's nurse. She is taking care of the baby, and no harm will come to her. Try and relax. You are ill, you have been in an accident.''

Her stomach churned sickly, her head pounded with pain, but she had to ignore that. She stared at him and showed her teeth. ''Why are you doing this?'' A sudden wrench released her seat belt, and Anna thrust herself to her feet.

Ishaq Ahmadi's eyes flashed with irritation. ''You know very well you have no right to such a display. You know you are in the wrong, deeply in the wrong.'' He stabbed a forefinger at the chair she had just vacated. ''Sit down before you fall down!''

With a little jerk, the plane started taxiing. ''No!'' Anna cried. She staggered and clutched the chair back, and with an oath Ishaq Ahmadi snapped a hand up and clasped her wrist in an unbreakable hold.

''Help me!'' she screamed. ''Help, help!''

A babble of concerned female voices arose from behind a bulkhead, and in another moment the hostess appeared in the doorway behind the bar.

''Sit down, Anna!''

The hostess cried a question in Arabic, and Ishaq Ahmadi answered in the same language. *"Laa, laa, madame,"* the woman said, gently urgent, and approached Anna with a soothing smile, then tried what her little English would do.

"Seat, madame, very dingerous. Pliz, seat."

"I want to get off!" Anna shouted at the uncomprehending woman. "Stop the plane! Tell the captain it's a mistake!"

The woman turned to Ishaq Ahmadi with a question, and he shook his head on a calm reply. Of course he had the upper hand if the cabin crew spoke only Arabic. Anna had a dim idea that all pilots had to speak English, but what were her chances of making it to the cockpit?

And if it was a private jet, the captain would be on Ishaq Ahmadi's payroll. No doubt they all knew he was kidnapping his own wife.

Ahmadi got to his feet, holding Anna's wrist in a grip that felt like steel cables, and forced her to move towards him.

The plane slowed, and they all stiffened as the captain's voice came over the intercom—

but it was only with the obvious Arabic equiv-
alent of ''Cabin staff, prepare for takeoff.''
Ishaq Ahmadi barked something at the hostess
and, with a consoling smile at Anna, she returned to her seat behind the bulkhead.

Ishaq Ahmadi sank into his seat again, dragging Anna inexorably down onto his lap.
''You are being a fool,'' he said. ''No one is
going to hurt you if you do not hurt yourself.''

She was sitting on him now as if he were
the chair, and his arms were firmly locked
around her waist, a human seat belt. The heat
of his body seeped into hers, all down her
spine and the backs of her thighs, his arms
resting across her upper thighs, hands clasped
against her abdomen.

Wherever her body met his, there was nothing but muscle. There was no give, no ounce
of fat. It was like sitting on hot poured metal
fresh from the forge, hardened, but the surface
still slightly malleable. The stage when a
sculptor removes the last, tiny blemishes, puts
on the finishing touches. She had taken a
course in metal sculpture at art college, and she
had always loved the metal at this stage, Anna

remembered dreamily. The heat, the slight surface give in something so innately strong, had a powerful sensual pull.

She realized she was half tranced. She felt very slow and stupid, and as the adrenaline in her body ebbed, her headache caught up with her again. She twisted to try to look over her shoulder into his face.

"Why are you doing this?" she pleaded.

His voice, close to her ear, said, "So that you and the baby will be safe."

She was deeply, desperately tired, she was sick and hurt, and she wanted to believe she was safe with him. The alternative was too confusing and too terrible.

The engines roared up and the jet leapt forward down the runway. In a very short time, compared to the lumbering commercial aircraft she was used to, they had left the ground.

As his hold slackened but still kept her on his lap, she turned to Ishaq Ahmadi. Her face was only inches from his, her mouth just above his own wide, well-shaped lips. She swallowed, feeling the pull.

"Where are you taking me?"

"Home." His gaze was steady. "You are tired. You will want to lie down," he murmured, and when the jet levelled out, he helped her to her feet and stood up. He took her arm and led her through a doorway.

They entered a large, beautifully appointed stateroom, with a king-size bed luxuriously made with snowy-white and deep blue linens that were turned down invitingly. There were huge, fluffy white pillows.

It was like a fantasy. Except for the little windows and the ever-present hum you would never know you were on a plane. A top hotel, maybe. Beautiful natural woods, luscious fabrics, mirrors, soft lighting, and, through an open door, a marble bathroom.

"I guess I married a millionaire," Anna murmured. "Or is this just some bauble a friend has loaned you?"

"Here are night things for you," he said, indicating pyjamas and a bathrobe, white with blue trim, that were lying across the foot of the sapphire-blue coverlet. "Do you need help to undress?"

Anna looked at the bed longingly and realized she was dead on her feet. And that was no surprise, after what she had apparently been through in the past few hours.

"No," she said.

She began fumbling with a button, but her fingers didn't seem to work. Even the effort of holding her elbow bent seemed too much, so she dropped her arm and stood there a moment, gazing at nothing.

"I will call the hostess," Ishaq Ahmadi said. And that, perversely, made her frown.

"Why?" she demanded. "You're my husband, aren't you?"

His eyes probed her, and she shrugged uncomfortably. "Why are you looking at me like that? Why don't you want to touch me?"

She wanted him to touch her. Wanted his heat on her body again, because when he touched her, even in anger, she felt safe.

He made no reply, merely lifted his hands, brushed aside her own feeble fingers which were again fumbling with the top button, and began to undo her shirt.

"Have you stopped wanting me?" she wondered aloud.

His head bent over his task, only his eyes shifted to connect with hers. "You are over-playing your hand," he advised softly, and she felt another little thrill of danger whisper down her spine. Her brain evaded the discomfort.

"Did you commission work from me or something? Is that how we met?" she asked. She specialized in Mediterranean and Middle Eastern designs, painting entire rooms to give the impression that you were standing on a bal-cony overlooking the Gulf of Corinth, or in the Alhambra palace. But what were the chances that a wealthy Arab would want a Western woman to paint trompe l'oeil fifteenth-century mosaic arches on his palace walls when he probably had the real thing?

"We met by accident."

"Oh." She wanted him to clarify, but couldn't concentrate. Not when his hands were grazing the skin of her breasts, revealed as he unbuttoned her shirt. She looked into his face, bent close over hers, but his eyes remained on his task. His aftershave was spicy and exotic.

"It seems strange that you have the right to

do this when you feel like a total stranger,"
she observed.

"You insisted on it," he reminded her
dryly. He seemed cynically amused by her. He
still didn't believe that she had forgotten, and
she had no idea why. What reason could she
have for pretending amnesia? It seemed very
crazy, unless...unless she had been running
away from him.

Perhaps it was fear that had caused her to
lose her memory. Psychologists did say you
sometimes forgot when remembering was too
painful.

"Was I running away from you, Ishaq?"

"You tell me the answer."

She shook her head. "They say the uncon-
scious remembers everything, but..."

"I am very sure that yours does," Ishaq Ahmadi replied, pulling the front of her shirt open
to reveal her small breasts in a lacy black bra.

She knew by the involuntary intake of his
breath that he was not unaffected. His jaw
clenched and he stripped the shirt from her, his
breathing irregular.

She wasn't one for casual sex, and she had

never been undressed by a stranger, which was
what this felt like. The sudden blush of desire
that suffused her was disconcerting. So her
body remembered, even if her conscious mind
did not. Anna bit her lip. What would it be
like, love with a man who seemed like a total
stranger? Would her body instinctively recog-
nize his touch?

She realized that she wanted him to make
the demand on her. The thought was sending
spirals of heat all through her. But instead of
drawing her into his arms, he turned his back
to toss her shirt onto a chair.

''What will I remember about loving you,
Ishaq?'' she whispered.

He didn't answer, and she turned away, de-
jected, overcome with fatigue and reluctant to
think, and lifted her arms behind her to the
clasp of her bra. She winced as a bruised elbow prevented her.

Her breath hissed with the pain. ''You'll
have to undo this.''

She felt his hands at work on the hook of
her bra, that strange, half electrifying, half
comforting heat that made her yearn for some-

thing she could not remember. She wondered if they *had* been sexually estranged. She said, "Is there a problem between us, Ishaq?"

"You well know what the problem between us is. But it is not worth discussing now," he said, his voice tight.

She thought, *It's serious.* Her heart pinched painfully with regret. To think that she had had the luck to marry a man like this and then had not been able to make it work made her desperately sad. He was like a dream come to life, but...she had obviously got her dream and then not been able to live in it.

If they made up now, when she could not remember any of the grievances she might have, would that make it easier when she regained her full memory?

As the bra slipped away from her breasts, Anna let it fall onto the bed, then turned to face him, lifting her arms to his shoulders.

"Do you still love me?" she whispered.

His arms closed around her, his hands warm on her bare skin. Her breasts pressed against his silk shirt as her arms cupped his head. He looked down into her upturned face with a completely unreadable expression in his eyes.

"Do you want me, Ishaq?" she begged, wishing he would kiss her. Why was he so remote? She felt the warmth of his body curl into hers and it was so right.

A corner of that hard, full mouth went up and his eyes became sardonic. "Believe me, I want you, or you would not be here."

"What have I done?" she begged. "I don't remember anything. Tell me what I've done to make you so angry with me."

His mouth turned up with angry contempt. "What do you hope to gain with this?" he demanded with subdued ferocity, and then, as if it were completely against his will, his grip tightened painfully on her, and with a stifled curse he crushed his mouth against her own.

He was neither gentle nor tender. His kiss and his hands were punishing, and a part of her revelled in the knowing that, whatever his intentions, he could not resist her. She opened her mouth under his, accepting the violent thrust of his hungry, angry tongue, and felt the rasp of its stroking run through her with unutterable thrill, as if it were elsewhere on her body that he kissed her.

Just for a moment she was frightened, for if one kiss could do this to her, how would she sustain his full, passionate lovemaking? She would explode off the face of the earth. His hand dropped to force her against him, while his hardened body leapt against her. She tore her mouth away from his, gasping for the oxygen to feed the fire that wrapped her in its hot, licking fingers.

"Ishaq!" she cried, wild with a passion that seemed to her totally new, as the heat of his hands burned her back, her hips, clenched against the back of her neck with a firm possessiveness that thrilled her. "Oh, my love!"

Then suddenly he was standing away from her, his hands on her wrists pulling her arms down, his eyes burning into hers with a cold, hard, suspicious fury that froze the hot rivers of need coursing through her.

"What is it?" she pleaded. "Ishaq, what have I done?"

He smiled and shook his head, a curl of admiring contempt lifting his lip. "You are un-

believable,'' he said. ''Where have you
learned such arts, I wonder?''

Anna gasped. He suspected her of having a
lover? Could it be true? She shook her head.
It wasn't possible. Whatever he might suspect,
whatever he might have done, whatever dis-
agreement was between them, she knew that
she was simply not capable of taking a lover
while pregnant with her husband's child.

''From you, I suppose,'' she tried, but he
brushed that aside with a snort of such con-
temptuous disbelief she could go no further.

''Tell me why you won't love me,'' she
challenged softly, but nothing was going to
crack his angry scorn now.

''But you have just given birth, Anna. We
must resign ourselves to no lovemaking for
several weeks, isn't it so?''

She drew back with a little shock. ''Oh!
Yes, I—'' She shook her head. He could still
kiss her, she thought. He could hold her.
Maybe that was the problem, she thought. A
man who would only touch his wife if he
wanted sex. She would certainly hate that.

''I wish I could *remember!*''

He reached down and lifted up the silky white pyjama top, holding it while she obediently slipped her arms inside. He had himself well under control now, he was as impersonal as a nurse, and she tasted tears in her throat for the waste of such wild passion.

Funny how small her breasts were. Last time, they had been so swollen with the pregnancy…hadn't they? She remembered the ache of heavy breasts with a pang of misery, and then reminded herself, *But that's all in the past. I have a baby now.*

"Do you think I'll remember?" she whispered, gazing into his face as he buttoned the large pyjama shirt. It seemed almost unbearable that she should feel such pain for a baby who had died two years ago and not remember the birth of the beautiful creature who was so alive, and whose cry she could suddenly hear over the subdued roar of the engines.

"I am convinced of it."

"She has inherited your birthmark," she murmured with a smile, touching his eye with a feather caress and feeling her heart contract with tenderness. "Is that usual?"

He finished the last button and lifted his eyes to hers. "What is it you hope to discover?" he asked, his hands pulling at her belt with cool impersonality. "The...Ahmadi mark," he said. "It proves beyond a doubt that Safiyah and I come of the same blood. Does that make you wary?"

"Did you think I had a lover?" she asked. "Did you think it was someone else's child?"

His eyes darkened with the deepest suspicion she had yet seen in them, and she knew she had struck a deep chord. "You know that much, do you?"

Somewhere inside her an answering anger was born. "You're making it pretty obvious! Does the fact that you've now been proven wrong make you think twice about things, Ishaq?"

"Wrong?" he began, then broke off, stripped the suede pants down her legs and off, and knelt to hold the pyjama bottoms for her. His hair was cut over the top in a thick cluster of black curls whose vibrant health reflected the lampglow. Anna steadied herself with a hand on his shoulder and stifled the whispering desire that melted through her thighs at the nearness of him.

They were too big. In fact, they were men's pyjamas.

"Why don't I have a pair of pyjamas on the plane?" she asked.

"Perhaps you never wear them."

He spoke softly, but the words zinged to her heart. She shivered at the thought that she slept naked next to Ishaq Ahmadi. She wondered what past delights were lurking, waiting to be remembered.

"And you do?"

"I often fly alone," he said.

It suddenly occurred to her that he had told her absolutely nothing all night. Every single question had somehow been parried. But when she tried to formulate words to point this out, her brain refused.

Even at its tightest the drawstring was too big for her slim waist, and the bunched fabric rested precariously on the slight swell of her hips. Ishaq turned away and lifted the feathery covers of the bed to invite her to slip into the white, fluffy nest.

She moved obediently, groaning as her muscles protested at even this minimal effort. Once flat on her back, however, she sighed with relief. ''Oh, that feels good!''

Ishaq bent to flick out the bedside lamp, but her hand stopped him. ''Bring me the baby,'' she said.

''You are tired and the baby is asleep.''

''But she was crying. She may be hungry.''

''I am sure the nurse has seen to that.''

''But I want to breast-feed her!'' Anna said in alarm.

He blinked as if she had surprised him, but before she could be sure of what she saw in his face his eyelids hooded his expression.

''Tomorrow will not be too late for that, Anna. Sleep now. You need sleep more than anything.''

On the last word he put out the light, and it was impossible to resist the drag of her eyelids in the semidarkness. ''Kiss her for me,'' she murmured, as Lethe beckoned.

''Yes,'' he said, straightening.

She frowned. ''Don't we kiss good-night?''

A heartbeat, two, and then she felt the touch

of his lips against her own. Her arms reached to embrace him, but he avoided them and was standing upright again. She felt deprived, her heart yearning towards him. She tried once more.

''I wish you'd stay with me.''

''Good night, Anna.'' Then the last light went out, a door opened and closed, and she was alone with the dark and the deep drone of the engines.

Five

"Hurry, hurry!"

The voices and laughter of the women mirrored the bubble of excitement in her heart, and she felt the corners of her mouth twitch up in anticipation.

"I'm coming!" she cried.

But they were impatient. Already they were spilling out onto the balcony, whose arching canopy shaded it from the harsh midday sun. Babble arose from the courtyard below: the slamming of doors, the dance of hooves, the shouts of men. Somewhere indoors, musicians tuned their instruments.

"He is here! He arrives!" the women cried, and she heard the telltale scraping of the locks and bars and the rumble of massive hinges in the distance as the gates opened wide. A cry went up and the faint sound of horses' hooves thudded on the hot, still air.

"They are here already! Hurry, hurry!" cried the women.

She rose to her feet at last, all in white except for the tinkling, delicate gold at her forehead, wrists, and ankles, a white rose in her hand. Out on the balcony the women were clustered against the carved wooden arabesques of the screen that hid them from the admiring, longing male eyes below.

She approached the screen. Through it the women had a view of the entire courtyard running down to the great gates. These were now open in welcome, with magnificently uniformed sentinels on each side, and the mounted escort approached and cantered between them, flags fluttering, armour sending blinding flashes of intense sunlight into unwary eyes.

They rode in pairs, rank upon rank, leading the long entourage, their horses' caparisons *increasing in splendour with the riders' rank. Then at last came riders in the handsomest array, mounted on spirited, prancing horses.*

"There he is!" a voice cried, and a cheer began in several throats and swelled.

Her eyes were irresistibly drawn to him. He was sternly handsome, his flowing hair a mass of black curls, his beard neat and pointed, his face grave but his eyes alight with humour. His jacket was rich blue, the sleeves ruched with silver thread; his silver breastplate glowed almost white. Across it, from shoulder to hip, a deep blue sash lay against the polished metal.

The sword at his hip was thickly encrusted with jewels. His fingers also sparkled, but no stone was brighter than his dark eyes as he glanced up towards the balcony as if he knew she was there. His eyes met hers, challenged and conquered in one piercingly sweet moment.

Her heart sprang in one leap from her breast and into his keeping.

As he rode past below, the white rose fell from her helpless hand. A strong dark hand plucked it from the air and drew it to his lips, and she cried softly, as though the rose were her own white throat.

He did not glance up again, but thrust the rose carefully inside the sash, knowing she watched. She clung to the carved wooden arabesques, her strength deserting her.

"So fierce, so handsome!" she murmured. "As strong and powerful as his own black destrier, I dare swear!"

The laughter of the women chimed around her ears. "Ah, truly, and love is blind and sees white as black!" they cried in teasing voices. "Black? But the prince's horse is white! Look again, mistress!"

She looked in the direction of their gesturing, as the entourage still came on. In the centre of the men on black horses rode one more richly garbed than all. His armour glowed with beaten gold, his richly jewelled turban was cloth of gold, ropes of pearls draped his chest, rubies and emeralds adorned his fingers and ears. His eyebrows were strong and black, his jaw square, his beard thick and curling. He lifted a hand in acknowledgement as those riders nearest him tossed gold and silver coins to the cheering crowd.

Her women were right. Her bridegroom was mounted on a prancing stallion as white as the snows of Shir.

"*Saba'ul khair, madame.*"

Anna rolled over drowsily and blinked while intense sunlight poured into the cabin from the little portholes as, *whick whick whick whick,* the air hostess pulled aside the curtains.

Her eyes frowned a protest. "Is it morning already?"

The woman turned from her completed task and smiled. "We here, madame."

Anna leapt out of the bed, wincing with the protest from her bruised muscles, and craned to peer out the porthole. They were flying over water, deep sparkling blue water dotted with one or two little boats, and were headed towards land. She saw a long line of creamy beach, lush green forest, a stretch of mixed golden and grey desert behind, and, in the distance, snow-topped mountains casting a spell at once dangerous and thrilling.

"Where on earth are we?"

"Shower, madame?"

"Oh, yes!"

The hostess smiled with the pleasure of someone who had recently memorized the word but had produced it without any real conviction and was now delighted to see that the sounds did carry meaning, and led her into the adjoining bathroom.

Anna waved away her offer of help, stripped and got into the shower stall, then stood gratefully under the firm spray of water, first hot, then cool. This morning her body was sore all over, but her headache was much less severe.

Her memory wasn't in much better shape, though. It still stopped dead on the night before she had been due to leave for France. Now, however, she could remember a shopping expedition with Lisbet during the afternoon, going home to dress, meeting Cecile and Lisbet at the Riverfront Restaurant. Now she could remember leaving the restaurant, and almost immediately seeing a cab pull up across the street. "You take that one, Anna, it's facing your direction,'' Lisbet had commanded, and she had dashed across the street...

She could remember *that* as if it were yesterday.

Of the two years that had followed that night there was still absolutely nothing in her memory. Not one image had surfaced overnight to flesh out the bare outline Ishaq Ahmadi had given of her life since.

When she tried to make sense of it all, her head pounded unmercifully. The whole thing made her feel eerie, creepy.

Last night's dream surfaced cloudily in her mind. She had the feeling that the man on the black horse was Ishaq Ahmadi.

She wondered if that held some clue about her first meeting with him. Had she seen him from a distance and fallen in love with him?

That she could believe. If ever there was a man you could take one look at and know you'd met your destiny, Ishaq Ahmadi was it. But he was definitely keeping something from her. If once they had loved each other, and she certainly accepted that, there was a problem now. It was in his eyes every time he looked at her. His look said she was a criminal—attractive and desirable, perhaps, but not in the least to be trusted.

Anna winced as she absently scrubbed a sore spot. The accident must have been real enough. Her body seemed to be one massive bruise now, and she ached as if she had been beaten with a bat.

That thought stilled her for a moment. Panic whispered along her nerves. Suppose a man had beaten his pregnant, runaway wife and wanted to avoid the consequences…

Anna reminded herself suddenly that they would be landing soon and turned off the water. In the bedroom mirror she stared at herself. She was still too thin, just as she had been after losing her baby two years ago. There were dark circles under her eyes to match the bruising on her body.

She had a tendency to lose weight with unhappiness. Anna sighed. By the look of her, she had been deeply unhappy recently, as unhappy as when she had lost Jonathan's baby. But the question was—had she lost the weight *before* she left Ishaq, or *after?*

Her clothes were lying on the neatly made bed. The shirt had been mended, the suede pants neatly brushed. Anna's breath hissed between her teeth. *It's terrific, Anna. Stop dithering and buy it!*

She had bought this shirt on that Friday afternoon and worn it that night to dinner in the Riverfront. These were the clothes that she could remember putting on that night. Her jacket was missing, that was all.

Anna stood staring, her heart in her throat. With careful precision she reached down and picked up the shirt. The tag was completely fresh. Either she was confusing two separate memories in her mind...or she and Lisbet had bought this shirt yesterday.

"Ah, I was just coming for you," Ishaq Ahmadi said, as she opened the door. "We are about to land. Come and sit down."

He sank into an armchair as Anna obeyed. Beside him the nurse sat with the baby in her arms. The air hostess was behind the bar. Anna could smell coffee.

"I'll take the baby," she said, holding out her arms.

To her fury, the nurse glanced up at Ishaq Ahmadi.

"Give me the baby," she ordered firmly.

Ishaq Ahmadi nodded all but invisibly, and the nurse passed the baby over. Safiyah was sleeping. Anna stroked her, the hungry memory of the son who had not lived assuaged by the touch of the tiny, helpless body, the feather-soft skin, the curling perfect hand. Her mouth, full, soft and tender, was twitching with her dream, as were her dark, beautifully arched eyebrows.

Anna glanced up at Ishaq Ahmadi and thought that he had probably once had the same mouth. But now its fullness was disciplined, its softness was lost in firmness of purpose, its tenderness had disappeared.

She wanted to believe that he was telling the truth. That he was her husband and that this was the child of their mutual love. She wanted to believe the evidence of the shirt was somehow false. Her heart was deeply touched by the baby, the man. It was possible, after all.

She might have packed the shirt away, left everything with friends, perhaps, and then, fleeing to those friends from her husband, had recourse to her old clothes.

Or confusing the memory of two different shopping trips might be a sign that her more recent memory was returning.

"Where are we?" she asked, watching out the window as the wheels touched down in the familiar chirping screech of arrival.

Palm trees, sunlight, low white buildings, the name on the terminal building in scrolling green Arabic script, the red Roman letters underneath moving past too fast for her to read...

"We are in Barakat al Barakat, the capital of the Barakat Emirates," he said.

"Oh!" She had heard of the Emirates, of course. But she knew almost nothing about the country except that it was ruled by three young princes who had inherited jointly from their father. "Is it—is it your...our...home?"

"Of course."

"Are you Barakati?"

"Of course," he said again.

She had some faint idea that amnesia victims didn't forget general knowledge, only personal. So how was it that she couldn't remember anything about the country that was her home? Her skin began to shiver with nervous fear.

A few minutes later the door opened. Bright sunshine and fresh air streamed into the aircraft, bringing with it the smell of hot tarmac and fuel and the sea and...in spite of those mundane odours, some other, secret scent that seemed full of mystery and magic and the East.

An official came deferentially aboard in an immigration check that was clearly token, and her lack of a passport wasn't even remarked on. Anna flicked a glance at Ishaq as the men spoke. Well, it wasn't surprising that he was as important as that. She could have guessed it just by looking at him.

Down below a sparkling white limousine waited, and the chauffeur and a cluster of other people were standing on the tarmac.

"Give the baby to the nurse," Ishaq Ahmadi said when the official departed with a nod and smile. Anna immediately clutched Safiyah tight.

"She's sleeping," she protested, with the sudden, nameless conviction that if she obeyed him she would never see the baby again.

"Give the baby to the nurse," he repeated, approaching her.

Anna evaded him, and stepped to the open doorway of the aircraft. "If you try to take her away from me, I'll scream. How far does your influence go with the people out there?"

Out on the tarmac her appearance in the doorway caused a little stir. People were gazing her way now.

Ishaq's jaw tightened and his eyes flashed at her with deep, suspicious anger. "How cunning you think you are. So be it."

He came up beside her and, with an arm around her waist, stepped with her through the door onto the top step. He stopped there, and to Anna's utter amazement, two of the men below produced cameras and began snapping photos of them.

"What on earth—?" she exclaimed.

She heard him murmur what sounded like a curse. "Smile," he ordered, with a grimness that electrified her. "Smile or I will throttle you in front of them all."

"What is it?" she whispered desperately. "Who are you?" and then, crazily, after a beat, "Who am I?"

"You will not say anything, anything at all, to the journalists."

"Journalists?"

She stared at the photographers in stunned, stupid dismay. What was going on? What could explain what was happening to her?

Ishaq went down the narrow stairs one step ahead of her, turning to guide her down. His hand was commanding, and almost cruel, against her wrist. In crazy contradiction to her feelings, the sun was heaven, the breeze delicious. Light bounced from the tarmac, the car, the planc with stupefying brilliance.

A man with a camera jumped right in front of them, and Anna recoiled with a jolt. "Excuse me!" she murmured, outraged, but he only bent closer. "Please, you'll disturb the baby!"

"Ingilisiya!" someone cried. *"Man hiya?"*

"Louk these way, pliz!"

The chauffeur had leapt to open the door of the limousine, and Ishaq shepherded her quickly to it. Before Anna's eyes could adjust to the blinding sunlight she was in the dimness of the car, the door shutting her and the baby behind tinted glass.

The voices were still calling questions. She heard Ishaq's deeper voice answer. A moment later he was slipping into the seat beside her. The nurse got into the front seat. The chauffeur slammed the last door and the limousine moved off as a cameraman bent to the window nearest Anna and snapped more pictures.

She turned to Ishaq.

"What's going on?" she said. "Why are there journalists here?"

"They are here because they permanently stake out the airport. The tabloids of the world like to print photographs of the Cup Companions of the princes of Barakat as they come and go in the royal jets. Usually it does not matter. But now—" he turned and looked at her with a cold accusation in his eyes that terrified her ''—now they have a photograph of the baby.''

Too late, she realized how foolish she had been to defy him when she knew nothing at all.

Six

The limousine turned between big gates into a tree-lined courtyard and swept to a stop in front of a two-storey villa in terra-cotta brick and stone with a tiled roof. The facade was lined with a row of peach-coloured marble pillars surmounted with the kind of curving scalloped arches Anna was more used to painting on clients' walls than seeing in real life.

Anna's heart began beating with hard, nervous jolts.

"Are we here?" she murmured, licking her lips.

It was a stupid question, and he agreed blandly, ''We are here.''

The door beside her opened. Anna got awkwardly out of the car, the baby in one arm. She stood looking around as Ishaq Ahmadi joined her. The courtyard was shaded with tall trees, shrubs and bushes, and cooled with a running fountain, and she had a sudden feeling of peace and safety.

''Is this your house?''

He bowed.

The baby woke up and started making grumpy noises, and the nurse appeared smilingly at Anna's side. She clucked sympathetically and made an adoring face at the complaining baby, then glanced up at Anna.

Anna resolutely shook her head and, with a defiant glance at Ishaq Ahmadi, shifted the baby up onto her shoulder. The baby wasn't going out of her sight till she understood a lot more than she did right now.

But he merely shrugged. A servant in white appeared through one of the arches, and they all moved into the shade of the portico.

Her eyes not quite accustomed to the cool

gloom, she followed Ishaq Ahmadi into the house, through a spacious entrance hall and into the room beyond. There the little party stopped, while Ishaq Ahmadi conversed in low tones with the servant.

Anna opened her mouth with silent, amazed pleasure as she gazed around her. She had never seen a room so beautiful outside of a glossy architectural magazine. An expanse of floor patterned in tiles of different shades and designs, covered here and there with the most beautiful Persian carpets she had ever seen, stretched the length of a room at least forty feet long.

There were low tables, sofas covered in richly coloured, beautifully woven fabric like the most luscious of kilims, a black antique desk, and ornately carved and painted cabinets. Beautiful objets d'art sat in various niches, hung on the walls, stood on the floor.

A wall that was mostly window showed a roofed balcony overlooking a courtyard, in which she could see the leafy tops of trees moving gently in the breeze. The balcony was faced with a long series of marble pillars supporting sculpted and engraved stone arches and walled with intricately carved wooden screens. Beyond the treetops, she saw a delicious expanse of blue sky and sea.

Anna closed her eyes, looked again. Heaved a breath. She felt the deepest inner sense of coming home, as if after interminable exile. She belonged here. She sighed deeply.

She turned to Ishaq Ahmadi. "Why was I in London?" she asked.

He raised his eyebrows in enquiry.

"I've been doubting you and everything you told me," she explained. She closed her eyes and inhaled, letting out her breath on another deep sigh of relief. "But I *know* this is home. Why did I leave, Ishaq? Why did you have to bring me home by force?"

He looked at her with an unreadable expression.

"Do you tell me you remember the house?"

She shook her head. "No...not really *remember*. But I have the feeling of belonging."

"You are a mystery to me," he said flatly. "Give Safiyah to the nurse, and let us have something to drink."

The manservant was waiting silently, and Ishaq turned to him with a quiet order. With a slight bow the man moved away.

Meanwhile, with a caress, a kiss and a lingering glance, Anna let the nurse take Safiyah from her arms. The woman smiled reassuringly and disappeared through a doorway, leaving Anna alone with Ishaq Ahmadi.

Who was opening a door onto the magnificent balcony. "Come," he said, in a voice that instantly dispelled her more relaxed mood. "We have things to discuss."

He slipped off his suit jacket and tossed it onto a chair.

She hesitated.

"My dear Anna, I assure you there is nothing to fear on the terrace," he said. "No one will throw you over the edge, though it is undoubtedly what you deserve."

What she deserved? Well, there was no answer she could make to that until she remembered more.

"Do I—have I left any clothes here?" Anna asked, rather than challenge him, feeling she could hardly bear any more wrangling. She couldn't remember ever having felt so tired. "Because if so, I'd like to change into something cooler."

"I am sure there is something to accommodate you. Shall I show you, or do you remember the way?" Then, correcting himself, "No, of course, you remember nothing."

She followed without challenging that mockery as he closed the door again and led her along half the length of the room and down a flight of stairs. There they walked along a hall and he opened a door.

If she had been hoping that the sight of her bedroom would trigger memories, that hope died as she entered the utterly impersonal room. For all the feeling that the room had been inhabited for centuries, there was not one photograph, one personal item on view. A few bottles of cosmetics on a dressing table were the only evidence that a woman slept here.

Well, she had known from the beginning that her marriage was troubled, so there was no reason to weep over this confirmation. Anna opened the door of a walk-in closet. Inside there were empty hangers, a few items in garment bags, a pair of sandals on the floor, a case neatly placed on a shelf.

So she had left him. She had preferred to run to London to have her baby in the back of a cab rather than stay with her handsome, passionate husband. Anna bit her lip. And he had come and kidnapped her and brought her back.

And she had no idea what that meant. Was she to be a prisoner now? Would he keep the baby and banish her? Or did he mean to try again to make a troubled marriage work?

She heaved a sigh, but there was nothing to be gained in trying to second-guess him. She was desperately disadvantaged by her memory loss, utterly dependent on him for any description of what had gone wrong between them.

Anna stripped, found some clean underwear in a drawer. Bathing her face and wrists in cool water, she paused and stared at her reflection. The face that looked back at her was not the face of a woman who was happy about having left her husband. Her eyes, normally a deep sapphire blue, looked black with fatigue.

Or perhaps it was the marriage itself that had done that to her.

The bra was too large for her. So she had been away some time? She abandoned the bra, slipping into briefs and a pale blue shirt and pant outfit in fine, cool cotton. The shirt was long, Middle Eastern fashion. It was size medium, and she had always bought petite. Anna shook her head. Nothing fit, in any sense of the word. One of the thong sandals was broken and she decided to go barefoot.

Ishaq, having changed his suit for a similar outfit to her own in unbleached white cotton, and wearing thong sandals, was waiting for her outside the door.

He led her up to the main room again.

"What time is it?" she asked as he opened the balcony door. He obediently consulted the expensive watch on his wrist.

"Eleven."

"It feels more like six in the morning to me," she remarked, yawning and stepping outside. "I feel as if I've hardly slept."

From here she could see that the house was built in a squared C shape, and the broad balcony she was on ran around the three sides. One storey below, the courtyard was deliciously planted with trees and shrubs around a fountain. Beyond that there were other levels of the terrace, connected with arches and stone staircases, but mostly hidden from view by the greenery.

"It is seven in the morning in London. We have travelled east four hours," he replied.

She laughed at her own stupidity. "Oh, of course! Well, it just goes to show how confused I am!"

"No doubt."

The balcony was partitioned with beautiful wooden arches in the most amazing scrollwork. As they walked through one of these archways, Anna paused to touch the warm, glowing wood. "I paint arches like this on the walls of rooms," she observed. "But I've never before seen the real thing at first hand." Then she turned with a self-conscious laugh. "Well, but except—"

"Except for the fact that you live here," he said blandly.

They strolled through another arched partition, past windows leading to magical rooms. The house seemed very old, the brick and tiles

well-worn by time and the tread of generations. Flowering plants tumbled in the profu-
sion of centuries over the balcony and down
to the terrace below, others climbed upwards
past the opening towards the roof.

"Is this your family's house?"

"I inherited it from my father early this
year."

"Oh, I'm sorry," she murmured, and then
shook her head for how stupid that must sound
to him—his wife, who must have attended the
funeral with him, formally commiserating with
him months after the fact.

"Sorry," she muttered. "It's hard to…"

Past the next archway a group of padded
wicker chairs and loungers sat in comfortable
array by a low table near a tiny fountain. Anna
sighed. Her weary soul seemed to drink in
peace so greedily she almost choked. There
were flowers and flowering bushes every-
where. The breeze was delicious, full of wonderful scents. The sound of running water was
such balm. The whole scene was luxuriously,
radiantly, the Golden Age of Islam.

"This is beautiful!"

As he paused, Anna stepped to the scroll-work railing and glanced down. She could hardly believe that any normal process of life had brought her to such a magnificent home.

The villa was not small. That was an illusion at the entrance level. Below her on various levels now she had a clearer view of the stepped terraces full of flowers and greenery, and discovered that the courtyard led to a terrace with an inviting swimming pool unlike any she had ever seen. It was square, set with beautiful tiles both around the edge and under water.

The house was built on a thickly forested escarpment above a white sand beach that went for miles in both directions. Straight ahead of her, across the bay, she saw the smoky blue of distant hills. To the left, several miles away around a curving shoreline, she could just catch sight of the city. Beyond the bay the sea stretched forever, a rich varied turquoise that melted her anxiety and fatigue with each succeeding rush of a wave onto the sand.

The murmur of voices told her that the servant had reappeared, and she turned to see him pushing a trolley laden with a large cut-glass pitcher of juice and a huge bowl of lusciously ripe fruit. All the glass was frosted, as if everything had been chilled in a freezer. In a few deft movements, the man transferred the contents of the trolley to the table, and at a sign from his master, retired.

As she sank onto a lounger Ishaq poured a drink and handed it to her without speaking. She put the ice-cold glass to her lips and drank thirstily of the delicious nectar, then lifted her feet onto the lounger and leaned back into a ray of sun that slanted in. The breeze caressed her bare toes. Behind her head a flowering shrub climbed up a pillar and around an arch, a carpet of pink blossoms. Anna smiled involuntarily as the heavy tension in her lifted. For a moment she could forget her fears, could forget how he had brought her back home, and simply be.

He sank into the neighbouring chair, facing her at an angle, leaned back and watched her over the rim of his glass. His gaze set up another kind of tension in her, that warred with the peace she was just starting to feel.

"So, Anna," he said. She closed her eyes against the intensity she felt coming from him.

"Ishaq, I'm tired. Can't we leave this for another day?"

"Delay would suit you, would it? Why?"

"I really am at a loss to understand you," she sighed. "I'm here, the baby's here, what else do you want?"

He smiled. "You have no idea what it is I want?"

"If I don't even remember being married to you, how can I possibly be expected to guess what you want?" she exploded. She could feel that she was very near breaking point.

"All right," he said. "Let us deal with what you do remember. As far as you remember, six weeks ago you gave birth and the child died."

She closed her eyes. There was no softness in his tone, and she wondered what kind of fool she had been to tell him, when she remembered nothing about what kind of man she had married. She must have had good reason for not telling him.

"That's how it feels."

"You were distraught over this loss."

"Yes, of course I was." She gave him a steady look, desperately hoping she would be able to hold her own against him. "And I remind you that you were not then part of my life, Ishaq."

"You wondered about the possibility of adopting a baby, but as a single woman you were not eligible through conventional channels."

"What?" She blinked at him. "I never said that! Why are you putting words in my mouth?"

"Anna, time is short. I intend to find the truth."

"The truth of *what?*" she exploded. "You keep telling me different things! How can you expect me to remember anything when you keep changing your story? What is it you want? Why is time short? Why are you playing these games? Why does the past matter now? It's over, isn't it?"

"You wanted a baby very much," he continued, as if she hadn't spoken.

"Ishaq—"

"You wanted a baby very much?"

"No, I did not want 'a baby' very much!"
she said through her teeth. "I wanted *my* baby.
My baby, Noah, who had every right to be
born healthy and strong. I wanted him. I still
do. You're going to have to face it, Ishaq. It's
not something that gets wiped out by time.
He's there in my heart, and he will never leave.
Safiyah joins him there, but she won't replace
him. Noah will always be in my heart."

It was the first time she had spoken of the
baby in such a way. Her urgency meant she
spoke without defending herself against the
pain, and her breath trembled in her throat and
chest. She felt the lump of stone in her chest
shift, and thought, *Six weeks of hiding from the
hurt is one thing. But what kind of marriage
can it be if I've been keeping this inside for
two years?*

He was leaning forward, close to her, but
staring down into the glass he held loosely between his spread knees.

"What drew us together?" she asked.

He lifted his eyes without moving his head.

"Have I never been able to be open about

my feelings before? Is our relationship entirely based on sex or something?''

His eyes took on a look of admiration laced with contempt. ''In spite of having no memory of me, you feel sexual attraction between us?''

''Don't you?'' she countered.

His look back at her was darkly compelling, and her skin shivered. There *was* a strong sexual pull. And if that was the centre of their bond, it would be foolish to pretend to exclude it from their negotiations.

He reached out and ran a lean finger along her cheek, and the little answering shiver of her skin made her heart race. ''Have you forgotten this?''

She gulped. Oh, how had she ever, ever managed to attract him? He was so masculine, so attractive, and yet with an air of risk, of danger. Like the powerful muscles under the tiger's deceptively furry coat, under Ishaq Ahmadi's virile masculinity there was a threat that he would make a bad enemy.

''It seems rather wasteful on my part,'' she agreed with a crazy grin, wanting him to smile without any edge. ''But I'm afraid I have.''

"Then I will have the pleasure of teaching you all over again," he said lazily. His hand cupped her cheek and he looked searchingly into her face. "Yes?"

She had no argument with that. She bit her lip, smiling into his eyes, nearer now. "It might even be the thing to bring back my memory."

"Yes, of course! That is the most ingenious excuse for making love that I have heard. But you always were imaginative, Anna."

His lips were almost touching hers, and her skin was cold and hot by turns. His hand cupped her neck and his fingers stroked the skin under the cap of hair.

She felt the rightness of it. She wanted to lean against him and feel the protection his strength offered, feel his arms clasp her firmly, feel herself pressed against his chest again. For in his arms, just as in this house, she knew she was home.

He moved his mouth away from hers without kissing her, moved to her eyelid. She closed her eyes in floating expectation, feeling the sun's heat and Ishaq's warmth as if both derived from one source.

He trailed light kisses across her eyelids, brushed her long curling lashes with his full lips, trailed a feathery touch down the bridge of her nose. His thumb urged her chin upwards, and her head fell back in helpless longing.

She felt starved for the touch, as if she had been longing for it for months. Years. Her arms wrapped him, her hand on his neck delighting in the touch of the thick hair.

At last he kissed her lips, and it was right, so right. As if some deep electrical connection had been made. She felt it sing against her mouth and melt her heart, and she felt his hand tighten painfully on her arm and knew that he felt it, too. Whatever had gone wrong between them, it was not this.

He was gnawing on her lower lip with little bites that sent shafts of loving and excitement through her. His other hand came up and encircled her throat, too, and he held her helpless in his two hands while his mouth hungered against hers, stealing and giving pleasure.

Anna pressed her hand against his chest, thrilling to the strength of heart and body she felt there. It was both new and old. She felt as if she had loved him in some long-distant past, some other life, and at the same time that it was all totally new. She seemed never to have been warmed with such delight by a kiss, never yearned so desperately for a man's love.

He wrapped her tight in his arms and drew her upper body off the lounger and across his knees with a passion that made her tremble. Now his mouth came down on hers with un-controlled longing, and he kissed her deeply and thoroughly until her bones were water and her heart was alive with wild, wild need.

His mouth left hers, trailed kisses across her cheek to her ear, down her neck to the base of her throat, and slowly back up the long line of her throat.

''Ishaq!'' She cried his name with passion-ate wonder before his kiss could smother the sound on her lips. ''Ishaq!''

His lips teased the corner of her mouth and moved up towards her ear.

"Tell me the truth, Anna," he whispered. "Tell me, and then let me love you."

"Tell you?" She would tell him anything, if only he would carry on kissing her. But she had nothing to tell. "Tell you what?" He did not answer, only stared compellingly at her, and she slowly turned away her head. "I don't remember," she protested sadly, feeling the passion die within her. "Why won't you believe me? What have I done to forfeit the trust you must once have had in your wife?"

His eyes squeezed shut, and she felt how he struggled for control of himself and bit by bit gained it. Then he lifted her to rest in the lounger again, took his hands away, and sat looking at her. She saw burning suspicion in his eyes.

"What is it?" she pleaded. "What do you want me to tell you? What have I forgotten?"

He shook his head, reaching for his glass, and nervously she picked up her own. He drank a long draft of juice, and set the glass down carefully.

"What have you forgotten, you want to know?" He looked at her levelly. "You have forgotten nothing, Anna. Except perhaps the humanity that is the birthright of us all. Tell me where Nadia is.''

Anna closed her eyes, opened them. Swallowed.

''Nadia?'' She repeated the name carefully. ''Who is Nadia?''

Ishaq smiled. ''Nadia, as you very well know, is the mother of the baby you kidnapped and have been pretending is your own.''

Seven

The storm of passion he had raised in her body was now a dry emptiness that left her feeling sick. ''What?'' An icicle trailed along her spine. She blinked at him, mouth open, feeling about as intelligent as a fish. ''What are you talking about?''

He watched her in silence. When she moved, it was to set her glass down on the table very carefully.

''I don't know anyone nam...the mother of the baby? Of Safiyah?'' Her voice cracked. ''She's not my baby?''

He was silent. She stared into his face. Was this the truth, or some kind of mind game?

"You're trying to break me," she accused hoarsely. "Tell me the truth. If you have any humanity at all, if you have one ounce of human feeling in you, tell me the truth. Is Safiyah our baby?"

"You know very well that she is not," he said. "Will you never come to the end of your play-acting? What can you stand to gain from this delay?"

Anna heard nothing except *she is not.*

"She's not?" she repeated. "She's not?"

He sat in silence, watching her, his sensual mouth a firm, straight line.

"If she's not mine, then...I haven't forgotten two years of my life, either," Anna worked out slowly. She wrapped her arms around her middle and looked away from his gaze, rocking a little. "And we aren't married, and this is not my home. It was all lies."

She looked into his face again, saw the confirmation of what she had said, and turned hopelessly to gaze around her. A quiver of sadness pierced her. It had seemed so right. Being here, the baby, the man—it had felt real to her. She shook her head. "But how…is one of us crazy?"

He looked like someone sitting through a badly acted play. "You, if you imagined you could get away with it," he offered.

Her mouth was bone-dry. One hand to her throat, she tried to swallow, and couldn't. "I don't know anyone named Nadia," she began, with forced calm. "I was in an accident and I woke up in hospital and they told me my baby was okay. You said you were my husband and I had amnesia. That's all I know. That is literally all I know."

Ishaq Ahmadi—if that was his name— leaned back in his chair. "You knew enough to pretend the baby was your own," he pointed out dryly.

She shook her head in urgent denial. "My memory was a complete jumble. You can't know what it's like unless you've experienced it. First I thought I was back at the time I was in hospital for…when my baby died. When they said, 'Your baby's fine,' I thought…" She stopped and swallowed. "I thought

Noah's death had been a bad dream. I thought I'd dreamt the whole six weeks since. I thought I had another chance.''

She forced down the taste of tears at the back of her throat.

''And then you came along,'' she said, in a flat voice. ''You turned everything on its head.''

It was all so crazy, so horrible, she could hardly take it in. She put a hand to her aching forehead. ''Where did the baby come from? Why did you tell me we were married?'' she demanded, fighting to keep sane. He'd be convincing her the world was flat next.

''For the same reason you pretended to believe me.''

''No!'' she cried. ''No! You know perfectly well—'' She broke off that argument, knowing it was futile. ''What is this? Why are you doing this?''

''You can guess why.''

She shook her head angrily. ''I can't guess anything! How dare you do this to me! Messing with my mind when I was concussed, telling me I was suffering from amnesia! What do you want? What can you possibly want from me? Why, *why* did you say she was our baby?"

"Because husbands have rights in such cases that others do not have."

She blinked at the unexpectedness of it. It was perhaps the first time he had given her a straight answer to any question.

"Are you the baby's father?"

He paused, as if wondering how much to tell her. "No. Nadia is my sister. "

"How did I come to be in the hospital with her baby? Did you plant her on me somehow?"

One eyebrow lifted disbelievingly. "Not I. That's what I want you to tell me. I found you there together."

Anna shook her head confusedly. "I don't understand. Then how do you know this is your sister's baby?"

"By the al Hamzeh mark." He rubbed his eye unconsciously.

"By the—*what?*" She jerked back in her chair. "Are you telling me that you abducted a baby and a total stranger from a hospital and brought us across four time zones on the strength of the baby's *birthmark?*'' she shrieked incredulously.

He gazed at her for a moment. Anna shifted nervously.

''Nadia was in labour and on her way to the hospital when she disappeared. A few hours later you turned up in another, nearby hospital, pretending to be the mother of a newborn baby with the al Hamzeh mark.''

''How did you know I *wasn't* her mother? The nurses told me it was my baby. So how did you know better? Is there really nobody else in the world with that mark except you and Nadia?''

''The nurse who examined you knew very well it was not your baby. She had written notes on your chart to that effect. You may read the notes, if you doubt me. I have them. She made a note for the hospital to check with the police for any reported incidents of baby stealing from maternity wards and to keep you in for observation till the matter was investigated.''

Anna blinked and opened her mouth in

amazed indignation. "But then why—but they—I *told* them my baby died, and they said, No, here's your baby, she's alive!"

He shrugged.

Anna couldn't fit any one piece of the puzzle with another. She shook her head helplessly, feeling how slowly her mind was working. "Anyway, if you knew I wasn't Safiyah's mother, why bother to abduct me? Why didn't you just take the baby? I wouldn't be likely to complain, would I, if I was faking it?"

"I wanted information from you. And you were in no state to—"

"Information about what?" she interrupted.

"About how you got possession of Safiyah."

This was unbelievable.

"Like for example?" she demanded. "What are you suggesting? That I—jumped Nadia while she was in labour, dragged her off somewhere, and then stole her baby when it was born?"

"That is one possible scenario, of course. Is that what happened?"

"Well, thank you, I'm starting to get a picture here,'' Anna said furiously. ''On no evidence whatsoever, you have decided that I am a baby snatcher. And that gives you the right to treat me like a criminal. You don't owe me an iota of respect, or the decency of truth. Nothing. Because of what you *suspect*. Have I got that now?''

Now she understood the reason for his questions earlier. The ugliest doubt of her own sanity brushed her. Was it possible? Had grief made her crazy enough to want a baby at any cost? Could she have done such a thing and forgotten all about it? Was that even the reason for her amnesia? No. *No.*

''And what do you imagine I did with Nadia?'' she went on, when he didn't speak.

''That is one of the things I want you to tell me,'' he said.

Anna leapt to her feet. ''How dare you talk to me like this? I did not do it! You have absolutely no grounds *whatsoever* for making such an appalling accusation!''

''I have not accused you. But you were in that cab with a newborn baby who is not your own. That needs some explaining.''

She was not listening. She stormed on. "How dare you take such extreme action on no evidence at all…lying, abducting me, making me believe I'm half crazy! Telling me… my God, and we almost made love!" she raged, her cheeks blazing as she suddenly remembered the scene.

"Was that my doing?" he asked dryly. "Or was that your attempt to get my guard down?" He was speaking as if this were only another such attempt. As if he believed nothing she said.

The flame of rage enveloped her, licking and burning till she felt something almost like ecstasy.

"Don't *you* accuse *me!*" she stormed. "*I've* never said anything but the truth! All the manipulation has come from your corner! You even lied about your name, didn't you? Last night it was the Ahmadi mark. Just now you called it the al Hamzeh mark!"

Ishaq Ahmadi looked bored. "Never lied to me? You lied to me not half an hour ago."

"I have not lied to you!"

He got to his feet, facing her over the

lounger, and Anna stepped back, but not fast enough to prevent his grasping her wrist.

"What do you call it? You told me you recognized this place, that you knew you had come home! You have not been within a thousand miles of this place."

Her eyes fell before the searching gaze. "Why did you say it?" he prodded.

She was silent. She had felt a sense of homecoming, probably only because she wanted to feel it. Wanted the baby to be hers, wanted him to be her husband. So desperately wanted all the sorrow and anguish of her terrible loss to be years in the past. There had certainly been enough clues that he was lying, if she had wanted to put them together.

"What did you hope to gain?" he pressed.

"Suppose you tell me!" she blazed, pain fuelling her anger in order to hide from him. She wrenched her wrist from his hold. "What advantage could there possibly be in saying something like that?"

"Perhaps you hoped to lower my guard and make your escape?"

"By sleeping with you, I suppose! Sexually

amoral, too. That's quite a charming list you've made up there.''

''You lied. You must have had a reason.''

''Dear Kettle, yours sincerely, Pot!'' she exclaimed mockingly. ''I have only your word for what's going on, you know. And your word hasn't exactly proved unassailable. You...''

She stopped. ''Why did you think I would believe you in the hospital, if things are as you say? You must have known I had amnesia. You must have been deliberately playing on the fact. Otherwise, why wouldn't I just tell the nurse you were an impostor?''

''I did not imagine that you would believe me. I thought you would prefer to pretend to do so, however, rather than run the risk of being revealed as a kidnapper and arrested by the police.'' Now she remembered that curious, warning pressure on her hand as she lay so dazed in the casualty ward. ''And I was right. You could not afford to make a stand, because that would mean an immediate inquiry. And any inquiry would have shown that the baby could not be yours.''

''If I hadn't been totally out of it I would

have made a stand soon enough,'' she said. She suddenly felt too weak to support her own anger. All her energy had been used up; she was empty. She had no more strength for holding pain at bay.

Her baby seemed to reach for her heart, the touch of that tiny soul unlocking the deepest well of grief in her. She shook her head and forced herself to confront Ishaq, to cloak her weakness from this dangerous adversary.

''If you hadn't lied about absolutely *everything*... If a lie is big enough, they'll believe it! Are you proud to be taking your lead from a monster?

Anger flickered in his eyes.

''I do what is necessary to protect those I love,'' he said coldly. She believed him. She saw suddenly that he was a man who would make a firm friend as well as an implacable enemy and, in some part of her, she could grieve for the fact that she was destined to be his enemy.

''Well, bully for you!'' she cried, her voice cracking with fatigue. ''I want to get out of here and go home to my life. So suppose you tell me what you want from me?''

Ishaq Ahmadi inclined his head. ''Of course. You have only to tell me where Nadia is and how you got her baby. Then you are free to go. I will of course pass the information and your name on to Scotland Yard.''

With a grunt of exasperation that almost moved into tears, Anna whirled to stride away from him. Against the wall of the house a railing protected a worn brick staircase running down to the courtyard below, and again she felt that crazy sense of belonging. *I have gone up and down that staircase a hundred times.*

She shook her head to clear it, stopped and turned to face him.

''Why don't you believe me?'' she demanded. He lifted an eyebrow, and she fixed her eyes on his. ''No, I really mean it. My explanation of events is as reasonable as anything else in this—'' she lifted her hands ''—in this unbelievable fantasy, so why won't you even give it a moment's consideration? You absolutely dismiss everything I tell you. Why?''

A sudden, delightful breeze whipped across
the terrace, stirring her hair and the leaves,
whipping the cloth on the table, snatching up
a napkin and carrying it a few yards. Her nostrils were suddenly filled with the heady scent
of a thousand flowers. The servant appeared as
if from nowhere to chase down the napkin.

"Because what you tell me has no logic
even of its own. How did you come to be in
the hospital with this baby?"

"Funny, that's exactly why I *believed* you,"
she said on a desperate half laugh. "How did
I get there? That's the question, all right."

"Your story has no foundation. It rests on
sand."

"What about the cab driver?" she exclaimed. "What did he say about it?"

"He was quite seriously hurt. He cannot yet
be questioned."

"Where did the accident happen?"

"The taxi pulled into the path of a bus on
the King's Road at Oakley Street," he replied,
as if she already knew. "You were in the back
with the baby. There can be no doubt of that."

She damned well was not, but she didn't

waste time on what he thought he knew. She wanted to sort this out.

"Oakley Street. That's only a couple of minutes from the Riverfront." The Riverfront Restaurant was moored near Battersea Bridge. "What time was the accident?"

"Not long after midnight, according to the police report."

She wondered how he had got access to the police report, but didn't waste time asking. "We asked for our bill around midnight, I'm pretty sure."

She squeezed her eyes shut. That meant her memory loss covered a very short period. If only a few minutes had elapsed from the time she got into the cab till the accident...

"If you're right, the only possible explanation is that the baby was in the cab when I got into it," Anna said, and as she said it, the truth finally pierced her heart. That darling baby whom she already loved was not to be hers to love...any more than her son had been.

Ishaq Ahmadi snorted. "Excellent. If only you had thought of this explanation a few hours ago."

Anna shook her head, swallowing against the feeling that was welling up inside her, a flood of the deepest sadness. She had no right after all to hold and love that beautiful, perfect baby, no matter how empty her arms were, how much she yearned.

''Perhaps a little later you will remember this. At a convenient time you will perhaps remember getting into a cab and discovering a baby cooing and kicking there.''

His words hurt her. *Noah,* she thought. *Oh, my baby! You never kicked and cooed....*

Suddenly all her defences were gone. She felt like a newborn herself. She dropped her arms to her sides.

''Maybe I didn't catch that cab. I don't actually remember getting into it. Drivers change shift around midnight, don't they? Maybe he wouldn't take me and we went up to the King's Road to try and get cabs there. Maybe...''

She was babbling. She didn't know if she was making sense. She blinked hard against the unfamiliar tears that threatened, against the sudden pressure on the wall that had held down her feelings for so long. She wanted to put her head back and howl her loss to the whole mad world that had let it happen, let her perfect baby die.

"Yes?" he prompted.

"I don't know," she said, despair welling up. How could she sort anything out when she could not remember? It was boxing in the dark. Was it possible she had forgotten some horrible conspiracy? Had her grief driven her to the madness of taking someone else's baby to fill her empty heart? Women did such things.

Tears began to slip down her cheeks. She couldn't seem to control them. Her head was pounding; it must be the heat. She staggered a little.

"I'm tired," she realized suddenly. "Really tired." She put out her hand to an arch for support, but it was further away than it seemed. A sob came ripping up from her stomach, bringing with it bile and the juice she had just drunk, and feeling came surging on its heels.

"Oh!" she cried. "Oh, I can't..." Her fingers caught at something, a branch, perhaps, but she couldn't hold on, and at the next sob her knees gave way.

The branch was Ishaq's arm. He caught her around the waist when she buckled, supporting her as grief and bile spilled from her amid howls of anguish.

"My baby!" she cried desperately, as the image of Safiyah blended with that of her own darling son, and seemed to be torn anew from her arms and her heart. Her throat opened, and at last she howled out the uncomprehending, intolerable misery that had been her silent companion for so many days and weeks. "Oh, my baby! My baby! Why? *Why?*"

Eight

———

''Princess, it is too dangerous!'' pleaded the maidservant. She stood wringing her hands as her mistress, gazing into the mirror, tweaked the folds of the serving girl's trousers she wore.

She glanced up, eyes sparkling in the lamplight. ''He is a brave man, the Lion. He will admire bravery. If I could, I would challenge him in the field of battle.''

''If anyone discovers you—''

''I will flee. And you will be waiting for me, with my own raiment,'' she said firmly.

She admired herself one last time in the mir-

ror. The short jacket just covering her breasts, the pants caught tight below the knee, the delicate gold chain around her ankles fanning out over her feet to each toe, the circlets of medallions around her waist and forehead, the glittering diaphanous veil that did not hide the long dark curls...the costume of her father's winebearers suited a woman well.

A smile pulled at her dimpled cheek as she turned away and kissed her maid. ''Fear not,'' she said. ''I am quick of mind and fleet of foot and I shall elude all save him I would have capture me.'' A delicious thrill rushed through her and she picked up the white rose that lay waiting and tucked it into her waist.

A few minutes later the two women crept together down the dark, secret passages of the palace towards the sounds of revelry in the great banqueting hall.

Inside the hall, the narrow doorway was hidden by a large carpet hung upright to provide a narrow passage against the wall, but as they glided in behind it, light from the banquet beyond revealed more than one spy hole in the fabric. She pressed her eye to one and gazed hungrily.

The men sat and lay around the laden cloth on cushions and carpets, drinking and eating, laughing, toasting the bridegroom, who sat beside her father. At the far end of the room musicians played. Serving men moved about the room, carrying huge platters massed with food. A whole roast sheep was being set down before the bridegroom.

But she had no thought for her intended. Her eyes searched the faces of the men seated nearest the prince, looking for the one they called al Hamzeh. The Lion. The birthmark made her search easy, even at such a distance, and her heart thudded in pain and delight as her eyes found him.

She took the golden pitcher from her frightened maidservant's hands then and glided stealthily out into the room, her movements measured by the bell-like tinkle of her jewellery. She walked down the room towards the Lion, as if in answer to a summons, as she had watched the cup bearers do.

He sat cross-legged on the carpet, leaning

against a mound of silken cushions at his el-bow, listening as someone described some feat of the bridegroom's at the hunt. His dark hair, glowing in lamplight, fell in tousled curls over the glittering gold embroidery of his jacket. On his fingers heavy carved gold held rich rubies and emeralds; high on his arm she noted the seal of his office, a signet in gold and amber. He seemed to glow independent of the lamp-light. She watched in a fever of desire as he bit into a sweetmeat and his tongue caught an errant morsel of powdered sugar from his full lower lip.

She approached, and bent over to fill the cup that he held in one strong careless hand. The scent of him rose up in her nostrils, spices and musk and camphor from his clothes, and from his skin the clean perfumed smell of a man just come from the hammam.

As if he sensed something in the winegirl, the Lion lazily turned his head and let his eyes follow the smooth arms up to her white breast, her half-hidden cheek. Instead of turning her face demurely away, she met his gaze with a look of passionate challenge. He started, his lips parting with questing amaze.

She let fall the white rose by the goblet, the little note fluttering like a lost petal from its stem. His eyes flicked to the rose, and she saw by his stillness that he understood. He turned and looked up at her, and now his gaze devoured the sweet face so passionately that her own eyes fell.

His hand moved possessively to gather up the rose before it could be noticed by anyone else—enclosing it jealously to keep it from other eyes, crushing it in a signal of all-consuming passion. She melted into answering passion as she felt his gesture on her own skin.

A thorn pierced his flesh and he smiled, as if a little pain was no more than to be expected from love.

Anna awoke in a strange bed and gazed around her.

Her headache was gone, and she felt deeply refreshed, as if she had made up for all the lost sleep of weeks past in one go. But the sunlight filtering through the shutters was still bright.

She had wept till she was completely drained and exhausted. She had wept it all out, for the first time, and then had fallen into a deep sleep. And now a burden had lifted from her. The heavy weight was gone.

Now healing could begin.

And of all people it was Ishaq Ahmadi who had sat beside her and witnessed her grieving. He had not said much, but his quiet presence had been exactly right. Someone to listen without feeling driven to reassure. Someone to hear and accept while understanding that nothing could be done to change her world for her.

With more interest in life than she had experienced for weeks past, Anna leaned up on one elbow and gazed around her.

She was in a different bedroom entirely from the one she had changed her clothes in. This was a very spacious room, beautifully decorated in blues and dark wood, with a door leading to the terrace. There were two other doors, and in the hopes that one of them led to a bathroom, Anna sprang out of bed and crossed an expanse of soft silk carpet woven in shades of blue and beige.

She got the bathroom first time, and when she returned to the bedroom, there was a smiling maid waiting for her. The bed was made as neatly as if Anna had never slept in it, and on the bed were laid clothes, as if for her choice.

"*Saba'ul khair, madame,*" the maid murmured, ducking her head.

Anna smiled. "*Salaam aleikum,*" she offered. It was the only phrase she knew in Arabic.

It was a mistake, because the woman immediately burst into delighted chatter, indicating the terrace beyond the windows and the clothes on the bed.

Laughing, Anna shook her head. "I don't speak Arabic!" she said, holding up her hands in surrender, but when she saw that among the offered outfits were several swimsuits, she turned towards the windows. The woman was opening the slatted wooden shutters so she could see more clearly what was out there.

The room was at one of the tips of the C. On the far side of the broad terrace was the swimming pool she had seen from above.

Ishaq Ahmadi was sitting at a table in a beach robe, reading a newspaper. A meal was being served to him.

Anna's stomach growled. She turned to the bed and picked up a swimsuit in shades of turquoise. It was beautifully cut and looked very expensive. Underneath that was another one, identical except for the size. With a frown of interest Anna picked up a few other items. Everything had been supplied in two sizes.

It might be conspicuous consumption, but as for refusing to accept his casual largesse, well, Anna was dying for a swim. So she stripped off her clothes and inched into one of the blue suits. It had an excellent fit, and she turned to examine herself briefly in a large mirror. She was thin, but the antique mirror was kind. Her shape was still unmistakably feminine. The suit emphasised her slender curves. The gently rounded neckline produced a very female cleavage, and her back, naked to the waist, had an elegantly smooth line. Her legs were lean but shapely, even if the large purple bruise on one thigh showed cruelly against her too-pale skin.

It was a long time since she had examined her reflection for femininity and attractiveness. Now it was perhaps a sign of her return to feeling that she was anxious to look attractive.

The maid held a cotton kaftan for her, and she slipped her arms into the sleeves with a murmur of thanks. It was plain white with an oriental textured weave and wide sleeves, and she knew without looking at the label that it had cost a small fortune. She chose a purple cotton-covered visor and a pair of sunglasses from a small spread of accessories.

He had thought of everything. He must have phoned a very exclusive boutique—or had one of his servants do so. Well, she would be glad if the utter stupidity of her trip here was relieved by a few hours of sun before she flew back to a wintry Europe. And though the items would be beyond her budget, they wouldn't amount to much for a man who owned a house like this.

The maid drew open the door for her, and Anna stepped out under the arched overhang and into the luscious day and walked across the tiled paving, past shrubs and flowers, past palm trees and small reflective pools, towards the swimming pool.

The air was cooler, and the sun had moved in the opposite direction to what she would have expected. She had thought the courtyard faced south, but in that case the sun was setting in the east.

Before she could reorient herself she had arrived at Ishaq's table beside the pool in a corner where the house met the high perimeter wall, nestled attractively under an arching trellis thick with greenery and yellow blooms.

He closed his paper as the servant pulled out a chair for her. A second place had been set.

"Good afternoon," she said, sinking down into it.

"Afternoon?" Ishaq queried with a smile, and she simultaneously took in the fact that his meal was composed of fruit and rolls.

"*Café, madame?*" murmured the servant, and she smelled the strong, rich odour and demanded, "What time is it?"

"Just after nine," said Ishaq Ahmadi.

"In the morning!" A breathless little laugh

of comprehension escaped her. "Have I slept an entire day?"

"I am sure you needed it. You must be hungry."

"Ravenous!" She flung down her sunglasses, then leaned back out of the shady bower so that the sun caught her face, and felt that she was happy in spite of everything. "Oh, this is heaven! What a wonderful place!"

He smiled. He had lost some of the hard edge of suspicion he had carried since they first met. And she—well, she had shown him things about herself that no one else in the world had seen. So it was only natural that she felt closer to him now.

He offered the basket of rolls. "Perhaps you would like what you call a full English breakfast?"

Taking a roll, Anna smiled up at the servant who was setting cream and sugar just so by her coffee cup. "I could devour a plate of bacon and eggs," she told Ishaq, then checked herself. "Oh, but—"

"I am sure the cook has some lamb sausage."

"That sounds delicious."

Ishaq translated her wishes to the servant. As the man slipped away, he said, "I do not ask my staff to cook pork for non-Muslim guests. I hope you will not object to doing without it during your stay."

"My *stay?*" She looked at him. "I want to go home. Are you planning on forcing me to stay here beyond today?"

"Force you? No," he replied calmly. "But you might reconsider when you look at this."

His hand was resting on the arm of his chair, holding the newspaper he had been reading. He lifted it to present her with the paper, front page up.

Trahie Par Son Milliardaire De Cheikh! screamed the French headline, which she could vaguely translate as *Betrayed By Her Millionaire Sheikh,* and Anna only shook her head. But then her eye was drawn further down the page, to a large photograph.

"That's me! That's you and me!" she cried in astonishment, snatching the paper without apology and spreading it under her horrified nose.

It was a photo taken at the airport, of herself, holding Safiyah, and Ishaq Ahmadi with one arm around her, guiding her to the limousine. An inset photo showed a sultry, big-lipped blonde whose face Anna vaguely recognized.

Very clearly marked—and too dark, so someone had obviously retouched the photo—was the al Hamzeh mark on the eye of Ishaq and of Safiyah.

"Oh, good grief!" Anna cried weakly. "Is this…" She glanced at the stack of papers on the table beside him, knowing the answer even as she asked. "Is it in the English papers?"

"Very much so," he agreed lazily.

She jumped up and ran to the stack. Of course, today was Sunday. The English Sunday tabloids were notorious for their love of scandal among the rich and famous.

Sheikh Gazi's Secret Baby!
Sheikh's Mistress In Baby Surprise!
Mystery Beauty Has Playboy Gazi's Baby!

All the tabloids save one had run it on the front page, with a variant of the photograph

she had already seen. Every headline insinu-
ated or said outright that the woman in the
photo was the sheikh's mistress and the mother
of his child. Worst of all, in virtually every
photograph Anna's face was clear and unmistakable. She looked exactly like herself. And
her arms were around the baby in a firm ma-
ternal hold that spoke louder than the headlines.

Still in a state of stunned disbelief, Anna
chose one of the papers and returned to her
seat, sinking slowly into it as she read the
story.

Sheikh Gazi al Hamzeh, the wealthy,
jet-setting Cup Companion and trusted
confidant of Prince Karim of West Barakat, startled the world yesterday with the
revelation that his long-time English mistress has given birth to his child.

The infant is thought to be over a
month old. ''The birth was kept secret till
Gazi could gain the prince's approval to
acknowledge the child,'' said a source
close to the sheikh.

Prince Karim, whose own son was born in July, is understood to be urging the sheikh to marry his so far unidentified mistress, seen here with the sheikh on arrival at Barakat al Barakat.

"Sheikh Gazi has gone to extraordinary lengths to protect the privacy of his mystery girlfriend," says our own society columnist, Arnold Jones Bremner. "Virtually no one outside his circle knows who she is."

Although the couple have been seen in some of London's most exclusive private clubs over the past year, they use a service entrance. This is the first photograph of them together.

Insiders say the couple are unlikely to marry.

Anna lifted her eyes to "Ishaq Ahmadi."

"*'Long-time mistress!'*—where did they get this?" she demanded. Her gaze hardened. "Is this what you told them?"

He laughed. "They did not trouble to ask me. The truth might have got in the way of invention. Suppose you had been the baby's English nanny! Where would their front page be then?''

''They asked you questions at the airport,'' Anna said stonily. ''I heard them. And you answered.''

His jaw tightened. ''Recollect that it was you yourself who insisted on presenting them with the tantalizing sight of the baby. But for that our arrival would have been unremarkable.''

''What does *Paris Dimanche* say?'' she asked, to catch him out. If the stories matched, surely that meant there had been one source?

He looked as if he saw right through her suspicious mind, but made no comment, merely lifted the paper and negligently began to translate.

''Sheikh Gazi al Hamzeh, the Hollywood-handsome, polo-playing millionaire considered one of the world's most eligible bachelors, has dashed the hopes and broken the heart of beautiful model/actress Sacha Delavel, his close friend, with the revelation that he is on the point of marrying the mother of his child. 'It comes as a total shock,' Mademoiselle Delavel reportedly told friends from the privacy of a villa in Turkey, where she is said to have fled as the news broke. 'I never knew of her existence until today.' ' ''

He tossed the paper aside as Anna's breakfast was placed before her. He deliberated over the fruit in the bowl and chose a ripe pomegranate as if he had nothing else on his mind. Then he neatly began to slice into the rind.

For some reason this story was much more infuriating than the other.

''I suppose when you're next seen with Sacha Delavel *I'll* be the one billed as having the broken heart,'' Anna snapped.

Ignoring her, he delicately, patiently prised open the pomegranate to reveal the luscious red rubies within. Anna shivered as if she were watching him make intimate love to another woman.

''Sacha Delavel and I danced together at a

charity ball given for Parvan war relief a few
months ago in Paris. They have searched their
picture library and found some nice photos of
the two of us, which are on page seven. The
rest is invention.''

She watched as he sank strong white teeth
into the red fruit. Liquid spurted from the seeds
over his hands and mouth, but he was concen-
trated on his pleasure. A thrill of pure sensation pierced her, and with a little gasp Anna
dropped her eyes to her own breakfast.

''Did they get your name right? You're
Sheikh Gazi al Hamzeh?''

''In the West I commonly use that name,''
he admitted wryly.

''Oh!'' she remarked with wide-eyed sarcasm. ''*It's* not your real name, either?''

''My name is Sayed Hajji Ghazi Ishaq Ah-
mad ibn Bassam al Hafez al Hamzeh,'' he
said, reeling the name off with the fluency of
poetry. ''But this is difficult for English speak-
ers, who do not like to take time over other
people's names. Nor do they trouble to pro-
nounce consonants that don't appear in
English.''

She couldn't think of any comeback to that. They ate in silence for a few minutes. With little flicked glances she watched him enjoy the pomegranate, and marvelled that anyone could believe that ordinary Anna Lamb was the mistress of such a powerful, virile, attractive man, or that he had dropped someone as beautiful as Sacha Delavel for her.

But she was pretty sure that people *would* believe it, now. It had been in the papers, after all. Probably even her own friends would wonder. Not Cecile or Lisbet, of course. But others less close to her.

"What do we do about this?" she finally asked, indicating the papers.

"Do?" Sheikh Gazi shrugged and wiped his hands and mouth with a snowy napkin. "Ignore it."

"*Ignore* it? But we have to make them retract. We could sue."

"And sell more papers for them."

"But it's all lies!"

Sheikh Gazi smiled at this indignation. "People will soon forget."

"But—aren't you going to do *anything?*"

"The editors hope that I will. Then they would have something to run with. A story denied is a story. Do you really want to see *Sheikh Gazi Denies Baby* as next Sunday's headline? Or do you prefer *Gazi Is Not The Father, Says Anna?*"

"But people will think—it says that you and I are…" She licked her lips and faded off, startlingly aware of the day, the heat, the luscious taste of fruit in her mouth, the smell of the sun on his skin. *They think we're lovers.* The thought hovered between them, shimmering like heat.

"And the more you say now, Anna, the more they will go on thinking it," he said.

"But I—I have to go back to London immediately. To France," she amended. "What if the papers find out my name?"

"They will certainly do so," he warned her softly. "As soon as the papers are read in London this morning—" he glanced at his watch "—it is nearly six o'clock there now—someone who knows you will call a journalist and name you."

They were reading the story before most

people in England were awake. She realized he must have some mechanism for getting the Sunday papers as soon as they rolled off the presses at midnight and flying them out to Barakat.

"Your price per copy must be astronomical," she observed dispassionately. "Do you have a regular Sunday delivery of the European papers?"

"No," he said.

The servant came with a new pot of coffee. He whisked their half-drunk cups away and poured fresh coffee into clean cups. Even with her worries, Anna had attention to note the luxury of that.

"Today was special, huh?" She had always dreamed of being famous one day, but for her work, not for something like this. "Well, so some friend or client will spill the beans. Then what? Will they phone me?"

"Phone you? They will phone you, they will phone your friends, they will come to your front door. At least one paper will offer you money for an exclusive, and if you accept, the editor will do everything to convince you to make the story of your sheikh lover more extreme and exciting.''

''What do you mean?''

''Before they are through you will be tricked or persuaded into confessing that we have made passionate, death-defying love in the back of a limousine as it drove through London and Paris, in moonlight on the deck of my yacht, high in the air in the royal jet, on the magical white sand beach down there, and even on the back of my favourite polo pony as it galloped through the forest. Naturally we have been insatiable lovers. And of course they will publish photos of you posed in my favourite piece of sexy underwear.''

His words sent electric twitches all across her scalp and down her spine, and Anna sat up abruptly and sugared her coffee. Was he being assailed by the same treacherous thought she was—that since everyone believed it anyway, they might as well make it the truth?

Nine

———

"**I**'m not going to be selling anyone any story," she said, setting the spoon in the saucer with a little snap. "Your polo pony's reputation is safe from me."

He lifted his hands in a shrug.

"But it really burns me that everyone I know is going to half believe I had your baby. What am I going to tell *them?*"

"That the story is false."

Her anger exploded on a little breath. "Oh, sure! You seem to forget that I actually have been pregnant. Only my close friends know my baby died. I haven't told anyone. I've

hardly seen anyone since it happened. Every-
body is going to wonder.''

He looked at her. ''I see.''

''And what happens when I don't have the
baby with me? People are going to think I
walked away and let you keep her.''

''Is it so bad? Fathers do get custody,'' he
pointed out, so offhand she gritted her teeth.
''And you have a career that takes you—''

She ground out, ''I would no more give up
my baby to its father for the sake of my career
than—'' She broke off with an exasperated
sigh.

''Blame it on me,'' he suggested. ''Every-
body knows Arabs are an uncivilized bunch of
barbarians who kidnap their own children.''

''Will you stop laughing at me?'' she demanded hotly.

''I will stop laughing when you stop being
foolishly outraged by something so unimpor-
tant. It is not the end of the world, Anna. People will accept that the story was false when
you tell them, or they will not. Either way they
will cease to care within a week. These
things—'' he flicked the pile of newspapers

with a gesture of such deep and biting contempt she flinched ''—they feed the lowest tastes in humans, and like any junk food the purveyors of it make it addictive and completely without nutrition in order to create a constant demand for more. One story runs into another in people's minds. It is a taste for scandal and outrage this feeds, not a desire for factual information.''

''I want to make them print a retraction,'' she said doggedly.

''Anna, by next Sunday, if we give them no more fuel for their fire, no one will remember whether you had a sheikh's baby or bribed a government minister, and no one will care! Do you know how many times my picture has appeared in these rags? Do you think anyone who gobbles such stories along with their Sunday toast remembers my name? I am 'that sheikh' if they think of me at all, and they confuse me with half a dozen other Cup Companions, or even with the princes themselves. Even with something like the al Hamzeh mark to distinguish me, people say to me, *Oh, you were in the paper, weren't you? What was that about again?* when the story was about the ex-Sultan of Bagestan.''

''You just told me a minute ago that they're going to chase me down like dogs,'' she said irritably.

''*Yes,* if you put yourself in their way.'' He gazed compellingly at her, lifting his closed fist, the first knuckle extended towards her, for emphasis. ''*Yes,* if you give them fodder by complaining. This is a story that has another one or two headlines in it at most—*if* we give it to them! If not, it will die now. This is not, as they say, a story with legs.''

''What does that mean?'' she asked doubtfully, half convinced. He seemed to know so much about it.

''To have legs? It is newspaper jargon. It means a story that is going to run under its own steam.''

She sat in silence, her chin in her hands, absorbing it.

''There is nothing to be gained by issuing a denial, Anna. The best you can do, if you wish it to go no further, is stay out of sight for a while.''

She tried again. "It's not as though I'm a celebrity, is it? It's you they're really interested in. If I can just get to France, I'll be fine. Alan's house is pretty remote."

"Let me offer you an alternative to France, Anna." His gaze was now utterly compelling. Although he was trying to disguise it, she realized that he wanted something from her, and the butterflies in her stomach leapt into a dance so wild she was almost sick.

She licked her lips. "And what would that be?"

"You could stay here with me until the heat dies down," he said.

A long moment of stillness was interrupted by the shrill cry of a bird in a nearby tree. Anna dropped her napkin by her plate with a matter-of-fact gesture.

"I—" she began, and then broke off. Her blood pounded in her stomach, making it feel hollow in spite of the meal she had just eaten.

"Do not turn me down without giving it some thought, Anna. There is advantage to you in staying away from the press for the moment.

And I assure you I will do everything in my power to make your stay enjoyable.''

Anna licked her lips. What was he really offering her here? A mere bolt-hole, or her very own Club Med holiday complete with dark lover? With any ordinary man, she would be in no doubt, but he was a man whose interest would flatter the most famous and beautiful women in the world. Why should he want her?

''For how long—a week?'' she asked.

He shrugged and lifted a hand. His hands were graceful and strong, and she wondered if he played a musical instrument. Or perhaps a man got hands like that playing music on women's bodies...she stomped on the little flames that licked up around her at the thought.

''Perhaps a week, a few weeks. It depends.''

On what? she wondered. Not on newspaper interest, obviously, when he had already assured her that would scarcely last till next Sunday.

Was he imagining that he would put her through her paces and see how long she kept him interested? She was unlikely to keep a millionaire playboy sheikh who hung out with the likes of Sacha Delavel interested for long. She had never studied sex as an art, and she would bet that he had.

"But people would find out I was here, wouldn't they? It would just confirm the story. So whenever I went back I'd have to face journalists wanting me to talk about it. Wouldn't I?"

He shrugged and plucked a grape from the bowl. She had the feeling again that he was hiding something.

"Where's the advantage in delaying the inevitable? At least if I go back now I can deny it. If I stay here even for a week no denial is ever going to sound credible."

It suddenly occurred to her that she sounded like someone wanting to be convinced, and she shut up.

"Can you think of no advantage from such a holiday? Barakat is a very exclusive holiday destination. No package tours come here. We have only a few resorts. That beach is as crowded now as it ever gets."

She couldn't refrain from a glance in the

direction he indicated. The strip of white sand curving around the bay in front of them was virtually deserted. So it actually wouldn't be stretching credibility too far to suggest that they had made love there, she found herself thinking absently...

Some part of her urged her to simply capitulate, and let nature take its course. But a little voice was warning her to be wary. Sheikh Gazi was not disinterested. What purpose would her staying serve for him? Was he really attracted to her, or was he deliberately letting her think so to disguise his real motives? And if he *didn't* want her sexually, what did he want?

Had he in fact been offering *her* sex as a bribe? He wanted her to stay and he knew she was attracted. Plenty of women would jump at the chance for a holiday in this paradise with a man like Gazi—and a sheikh, too!—devoting himself to them. Was he assuming she was one of them?

Anna, examining the grape between her fingers with minute fixity, blushed to the roots of her hair. After a moment she slipped it into her mouth.

"I would of course reimburse you for your time," he said, and that certainly proved the suspicion. He was simply trying whatever was handy by way of a bribe. If sex wasn't enough, he would throw in cash. God, what that said about his opinion of her!

"Really," she observed, her voice distant, almost absent.

"At your professional rate, of course."

She flicked him a look. "Which profession would that be?"

He chose to ignore the irony. "Which profession? I don't—you are an artist, you say. Artist, designer, interior decorator, whatever fees are your usual fees."

"Since you're doing me the big favour by allowing me to hide here, I don't really see why *you* should pay *me,*" Anna said sweetly. "Isn't the shoe on the other foot? Or perhaps you have some reason of your own for wanting me to stay?"

He sat for a moment tapping a thumb on his cup, considering.

"Yes," he said at last. "I also have reasons for wishing it."

"Well, well! And what would those reasons be?"

"I cannot discuss it with you," he said. The look in his eyes was an assessment, but a long way from sexual assessment. She realized abruptly that he did not trust her, or fully accept her version of events, even now. But he might be willing to make love with her if that was what it took to keep her here. Rage swept her, with a suddenness that astonished her.

"Suppose I take a stab at guessing?"

He watched her.

"Let's see, now," she began. She tilted her head and looked at him. "You're sure about that judgement, are you—that this story hasn't got legs, as you call it?"

"That a Cup Companion has a child with his mistress may offend the religious in Barakat, but for a Western audience it means nothing. You must be aware of the truth of this. As you pointed out, you are not a celebrity yourself. That gives the story only limited interest."

She nodded thoughtfully. "That's okay as far as our affair and our secret baby go, but that's all lies anyway. But there's something you're leaving out of the calculation, isn't there? I mean, that's not the only story here, not by a long way.''

She saw a flicker of feeling in his eyes, instantly veiled. He fixed her with a dark, impenetrable gaze. ''And what else is there?''

Anna did not stop to consider how unwise it might be to show such a man how thoroughly she understood his motives.

''You abducted a baby from an English hospital, Sheikh Gazi—and according to the papers, you're one of the trusted Cup Companions of Prince Karim. That's got legs, don't you think? You also abducted an Englishwoman. And you got us out of England and into Barakat without passports. That's got legs, too. In fact, it's got so many legs it's a centipede.

''And forgive me if I suggest that you wouldn't have done any of that just for sheer amusement. So the real reason you took such risks, Sheikh Gazi, whatever it is—that's a story that'll have legs, too.''

*   *   *

He was silent when she finished, and her ears were suddenly filled with the thunder of her own agitated heartbeat. Too late, Anna reflected that perhaps her reasoning processes hadn't fully recovered from her accident. What on earth had made her challenge the man here on his own ground?

"How well you grasp the facts," Sheikh Gazi said softly, tossing his napkin down beside his plate. "But I advise you to consider a little longer before you try to blackmail me, Anna."

His eyes were absolutely black. His gaze stabbed her, and her heart pounded hard enough to make her sick.

"I am not trying to blackmail you!" she shouted, rejecting her own dimly realized understanding that her little summation might well have sounded like it. "Why are you constantly accusing me of the lowest possible crimes?"

"What, then?" he said, his lips a tight line in a face that suddenly seemed sculpted from stone. "Just a pleasant little gossip to pass the time of day with me?"

She gritted her teeth. "Tell me, is it your wealth and position that give you the right to trample over other people, or is it just that women in general are beneath contempt?"

"I do not hold women in contempt," he said in flat repudiation.

"I have a life," she interrupted rudely before he had finished. "Forgive me if I find it offensive to be offered a holiday on the casual assumption that my career can be put on hold in order to save you from the consequences of your own actions." She tilted her head.

"I also resent being taken for such a fool. It's not me who's going to suffer if I deny this ridiculous story, is it? It's you. I have nothing at all to fear from the truth. Now—" She held up her hands. "I have no intention of telling anyone anything, except that you are not my lover and I am not the mother of your baby. But I do intend to get out of here and back to my own life. So unless you're considering adding forcible confinement to the list of your crimes—"

"You are annoyed because I have underestimated your intelligence," he interrupted with a sudden return to reasonableness that secretly irritated her. "Fair enough, but if you can see so far, a little more thought will tell you—"

"Please don't spell out anything more for poor little me," Anna snapped, lifting a hand. "I really think I understand enough. The rest I don't want to know. You might decide at some future date that I am a danger to you if I learn any more now."

His face closed, and she saw that he could be deeply ruthless when he chose.

"You are determined to consider only your own convenience."

"Me?" She could hardly speak for outrage. With biting sarcasm, she began, "I quite understand that *you* feel your concerns should come first with everyone you meet, Sheikh Gazi—no doubt it follows from having more servants than is good for you. But forgive me if *I* consider it quite reasonable that I should put myself and my clients first."

He gazed at her for a moment. "My concern is for my sister," he said quietly. "Let me—"

She lifted her hands, pushing the palms towards him. "Well, that's admirable! But I have already told you I know nothing about your sister. She is a total stranger to me. And my life has been quite disrupted enough on her behalf, thank you! Now I'd like to get it back on the rails.''

Sheikh Gazi acknowledged this with a hard, businesslike little nod. ''Let us hope that future generations consider such devotion to your art a worthwhile sacrifice.''

''It's no sacrifice on my part, believe me!'' Anna exclaimed explosively, if not quite truthfully. ''Not that I would *begin* to suggest that you rate your claims too high!''

He went absolutely still with fury. For a moment they stared at each other. Anna's skin twitched wildly all over her back and breasts as emotion flared in him, and she wondered what her reaction would be if he reached for her. If he started to make love to her, it was entirely possiblc shc'd end up agreeing to anything he asked her to do, short of murder.

As if in answer to her thoughts, Sheikh Gazi shoved back his chair and got to his feet. He shrugged out of his bathrobe, letting it fall onto the chair. Then he stood there, naked except for a neat black swimsuit in body-hugging Lycra. She could not avert her fascinated gaze.

Wind seemed to blow up out of nowhere, seducing all the flowers on the trellis overhead to give up their perfume, tousling her hair and robe, caressing her skin, so that all at once her whole body came alive.

He was gorgeous—there was just no other word. Beautifully proportioned legs, powerful thighs, neat-muscled waist curving up to a very male expanse of chest with just the right amount of curling black hair, broad shoulders that were held with the minimum of tension, strong arms.

Probably she would never get another chance at such death-defying sexual excitement as he had just offered. When she was an old woman probably she would look back on this day and call herself seventeen kinds of fool for turning him down.

Her gaze locked with his, her heart jumping, her stomach aquiver. She was acutely aware that the bed she had spent the night in was only yards away across the terrace.

He could convince her to stay. Even knowing his passion was totally calculated, a payment for services rendered, she would still burn up if he touched her. The thought of him using his sexual expertise to reduce her to willing cooperation in his plans, whatever they were, made her legs weak.

Sheikh Gazi al Hamzeh's lips parted. ''Then you will not wish to avail yourself of my offer,'' he said, with bone-chilling politesse. ''I will arrange for your return to London as soon as possible.'' Then he turned, stepped to the edge of that delightful pool, and dove in.

Ten

It wasn't as easy as that. Anna would of
course not be allowed to re-enter Britain without a passport. Her passport was in London,
however, in her flat. The keys to her flat were
in her handbag, which was presumably still at
the hospital. Before anything else, someone
had to be nominated to go to the hospital and
pick up her belongings, then go to her flat, find
her passport, and send it to her.

Anna wanted to ask Lisbet to do it, but
Sheikh Gazi frowned when she suggested it.
''The hospital must be dealt with very diplo-

matically. And anyone going into your flat may be questioned by journalists,'' he warned.

''Lisbet's an actress. She'll know how to handle that.''

''Allah!'' he murmured in horrified tones. ''You surely do not want someone to whom publicity is the breath of life being asked by the press about your private life?''

''Lisbet won't say anything. If anyone is going to be rooting around my flat in my absence, I'd rather it was Lisbet,'' she said doggedly.

''And your other friend—Cecile?''

''If Cecile was challenged by a reporter, she'd collapse and give them my entire life back to when I sucked my thumb, and be under the impression that she had handled them very well. I love her, but really, she just has no idea.''

''There must be another way,'' said Sheikh Gazi. ''I will consider.''

Anna had to insist on being allowed to call her client to explain her delay. ''What is the point? You will be there in a day or two,'' Sheikh Gazi argued.

''The point is I was due there yesterday,''

Anna said, thinking how different the percep-
tion of time was in the Barakat Emirates. It
was true there was no one at the villa to worry,
but what if Alan phoned from London and got
no answer? A day or two was plenty of time
to get worried.

Sheikh Gazi gave in very gracefully when
she explained how Sunday meant Sunday to
the English, and a delay till Tuesday or even
Wednesday was significant.

"Of course, darling. Whenever," Alan
Mitching said when she tried to explain. "You
relax and enjoy yourself. The villa's not going
to disappear. No one's using the place till
Christmas. You can get the keys from Madame
Duval anytime." She had the feeling that Alan
was sitting there with a tabloid leaning against
his breakfast teapot, avidly reading about her
and Gazi.

"Will you tell Lisbet that I'll be in touch?"

"Of course."

Having won this argument, Anna found it
harder to press the other. So when Sheikh Gazi
suggested that it would be best for someone
from the Barakati Embassy in London to get

her passport, since they could put it in the diplomatic pouch, she felt almost obliged to be as gracious as he had been in giving in.

He insisted on her being examined by a specialist, in spite of the fact that she would be back in London within a day or two and could see her own doctor. Although the man spoke German and French, he knew so little English Gazi had to translate for him.

"He says you are well, there is no lasting damage," Gazi told her, and she suddenly discovered, by the depths of her own relief, how frightened she had been, and was grateful to him for insisting.

Two days later, when she was expecting to hear that her passport had arrived in that day's diplomatic pouch, word came through that the hospital would not give up her handbag without a signed authorization.

It seemed things were going to move at a Middle Eastern speed. It was hard to find the energy to push for a faster conclusion, though, especially as the surroundings were so blissful. Her fatigue seemed to be taking this opportunity to catch up with her. Anna found she had

no physical energy for anything but swimming, lying in the sun, or wandering around
the beautiful house, and no mental energy at
all.

She signed a permission and Sheikh Gazi
sent it off by special messenger, and another
day drifted past like the others.

*The desert sky was black as a cat, with a
thousand eyes. The wind blew, hot and mad-
dening, around the turrets, driving her thin
robe against her body, biting sand against her
cheeks and into her eyes. She crept precariously along the parapet, feeling how the wind
clutched at her, trying to fling her down.*

*He was there before her with a suddenness
that made her gasp, his arms around her,
dragging her against himself.*

"You came," he whispered hoarsely.

*The wind whipped at her, but not so harshly
as his passion. Her back arched over his arm
as her eyes glowed up into his. "How could I
not?" she half laughed, half wept. "Am I not
lost, and are not you the polestar? Am I not
iron, and you the lodestone?"*

Holding her with one powerful arm, he bent over her and tenderly drew the scarf from her mouth to gaze at her face in the moonlight. He drank in her beauty with a hunger that melted her, his eyes burning with desire.

"How beautiful thou art," he murmured, and his hand captured one of hers and drew it to his mouth. He pressed the fingers, then the palm, against his burning lips, water in the desert.

He kissed her throat, white in the moonlight, and she trembled with her first taste of such passion. His eyes pierced hers again. "Thou art no slave girl!" he said.

She smiled. "No. No slave girl."

"Tell me thy father's name, and I will send to him for thee. I will make thee my wife."

She shook her head. "Thou art the trusted companion of a prince," she whispered. "And truly, I am no better than a slave. Do not seek to know my father, but only know that I willingly give up all for one taste of thy love. The world holds nothing for me."

He bent his head and his mouth devoured hers with a violence of passion. The wind gusted with a sudden fury, dashing sand cruelly against them. He tore his mouth from hers.

"Your lips are nectar. Tell me thy father's name, for I will not take thee like a slave, but wed thee in all honour."

"Ah, do not ask, Beloved!" she pleaded, but when he insisted, she smiled sadly and said, "Mash'Allah! My father is King Nasr ad Daulah."

He stared at her. "But the king has only one daughter! The Princess Azade, and she—"

"True, oh Lion! Three days hence the Princess Azade is destined to become the wife of the prince to whom you are sworn in allegiance. But for one taste of your love she forsakes all."

The baby was a source of deep delight. Safiyah seemed to have cast off the trauma surrounding her birth completely. She was a happy, deep-thinking spirit who loved to lie with Anna on the terrace under a flowery, shady trellis and watch the blossoms just overhead dance in the constant, cooling breeze.

"There couldn't be a better crib toy," Anna

told Sheikh Gazi. Because, whatever their differences, they were united in a deep fondness for the baby. ''It's even got musical effects.'' The birdsong from the trees planted around the terrace and the forest beyond was nearly constant, and it was clear from Safiyah's expression that she loved to listen.

Anna was picking up a little Arabic from the nurse, in the usual women's exchange of delight and approval with a baby. *Walida jamila* was the first expression she learned. She was pretty sure it meant *pretty baby,* and she and the nurse could say it back and forth to each other, and to the baby herself, with endless delight.

And every day she felt a little more of her long-standing fatigue and unhappiness being leached out of her body and self by her surroundings.

The only fly in the ointment was Sheikh Gazi himself. His job had to be very fluid, because he worked from home, and he was almost constantly around. He sat beside the pool in his trunks, tapping away at his laptop or talking into a dictaphone or telephone, while

Anna swam and sunned and played with the baby. She was constantly aware of him.

They ate together at nearly every meal. He had a powerful radio, on which he regularly listened to the news from several countries, and in different languages. They often discussed what was happening in the world, and although he was insightful and seemed very informed, he always listened to her opinions with respect.

He talked only a little about himself, though. When she asked, he told her that his job was to coordinate the publicity and public relations side of West Barakat's trade relations with the world, but spoke little more about it. Instead he talked about Barakat's history and culture.

He played music softly as he worked. Anna, who had rarely listened to Middle Eastern music, found it haunting, and in some mysterious way perfect for her surroundings. At intervals, too, could be heard from the city the wail of the muezzin, the Islamic call to prayer, and it all seemed to fit into one marvellous whole.

Sometimes it seemed as if the accident had been a doorway to another reality. A curious little space-time warp had appeared, and she had been shunted through—into some other life stream, where she joined up with a different Anna. An Anna who had made a different choice long ago, and now belonged here. Sometimes it seemed just as if Gazi had been telling the truth—as if they had been married for years.

Except for one thing.

However delicious the weather, however exotic the food his servants brought them, however sexy he looked emerging from the pool, his strong body rippling and his smoky amber skin beaded with water, however electrically she felt his presence—he never again suggested to Anna, by word or by deed, that her holiday out of time might include him as a lover.

He seemed totally immune to her physical presence. Whatever had made him kiss her with such passionate abandon on two occasions, he wasn't interested now.

She had never before met a man who had given up a pursuit of her after one little rejection, but that was what Gazi had apparently done. Or maybe it was simply that, in turning down his request to stay, she had lost her chance at the free lovemaking. In short, since she had refused his actual invitation to stay and was here only from necessity, he didn't feel obliged any longer to pretend he wanted to make love to her.

In every other way, they were practically the ideal family.

The fact that the constant delay getting her passport meant she had ended up staying after all never was mentioned between them. Anna sometimes wondered what his reaction would be if she made the suggestion that since she was, however inadvertently, acceding to his demands, he ought to live up to the original offer.

If you left out of the reckoning a teenage crush on a rock star, it was the first time in her life that she had felt such powerful romantic interest in a man who felt none in return, and it wasn't a sensation she enjoyed. Half the time she was determined not to accept even if he did change his mind, and the other half she had to restrain herself from making a clear pass.

He really was moving heaven and earth in the effort to understand her concept of time, and when she reminded him that another day was passing, he shook his head in frustration with his own stupidity and picked up the phone at once. But unfortunately, he was met with the same lack of focus at the other end. He ended up shouting in outraged impatience down the phone to a Barakati Embassy employee and hung up cursing.

"They understand nothing, these government employees!" he exploded. "To them nothing can be done without the correct documentation and by following established procedure! The person who collected your keys from the hospital put them in the safe last night, and today there is no one in the embassy to give permission for opening this safe." He glanced at her hesitantly. "I can phone Prince Karim, Anna. He is very absorbed with certain affairs of state, but...if I explain, he would call and order them to open the safe. Shall I do this?"

Anna blushed. "No, no, of course not! You can't bother the prince for that!" she exclaimed. And although he hid his relief, she could tell that it was not a request he had wanted to make.

And so another day slipped away.

Though she had told him she wouldn't be here long enough for it to be necessary, Gazi had been adamant about providing her with clothes suitable for the climate. So she had chosen a small but lovely wardrobe of mixed Middle Eastern and Western clothes from a selection sent in for her approval by a couple of city boutiques.

During the day she often wore nothing more than a bathing suit under a cotton kaftan. She never left the house, but for the moment she had no desire to do so, and it was great to be able just to slip off the kaftan any time and dive into the delicious pool.

The water was salt because the pool was, in accordance with Barakati law, Gazi told her, supplied by the ocean and not from the limited fresh-water resources of the country. So there was no smell of chlorine hovering over the garden or on her skin, and it felt like bathing in a natural pool.

She loved the sun, and although in this climate she was careful with exposure, she knew it was a source of deep healing. Her pale skin was a mark of her unhappiness and ill health, and she was delighted when it turned a soft brown.

The healthier she felt, the more physically she responded to Sheikh Gazi's constant presence, reading, tapping into the computer, talking on the phone. Sometimes she would lie on her lounger feeling the sun's hot caress and feel such a surge of desire for him she was convinced he was on the point of coming over to her, but when she glanced over he usually wasn't even looking at her. Or if he was, his face was tight with disapproval.

Every evening Anna dressed for dinner with the casual elegance her new clothes allowed. Made herself as beautiful as she could, without ever fooling herself she was competition for anyone like Sacha Delavel. She was being a fool, she knew, but she couldn't help wanting to see in his eyes, if only once, that she was attractive enough to disturb him.

Sometimes she would remember those moments when he had kissed her. She had felt such passion in his arms and his mouth, seen such burning desire in his eyes, that she had responded by going almost out of her skull with delight.

But now she had to wonder if that had been entirely faked. If he had merely been offering her a sample of the treats on offer. No doubt he could fake the whole thing if necessary. But she never felt that intensity in him now…and she found that was what she really wanted. She wanted to know she could touch his mind, his heart, his feelings. Not simply that he could perform a sexual service like a gigolo, if she insisted. That was how she stopped herself making a move.

They talked and laughed together over the delicious, candlelit meals until she was weak with wanting him. She was almost sure that the dark fire she sometimes surprised in his eyes held admiration.

Sometimes she couldn't believe that things

he said could be anything other than a prelude to lovemaking. But if so, his feeling never lasted more than a brief moment. Although she was somehow kept in a constant fever of anticipation and wishing, he never touched her. And if she touched him, even with a spontaneous pat on the arm as she spoke, he would stiffen and look at her with an unreadable look that made her lift her hand.

It didn't help her get a handle on her feelings to discover Gazi was the best listener she had ever met in her life. He drew her out as if he was really interested in her life and her opinions, her experiences and her dreams. He showed particular interest in her art, wanting to know what had drawn her to want to reproduce Middle Eastern art on the walls of England's houses.

The house itself was like the magician's cave, with masterpieces of ancient scrollwork and sculpture in every corner. The patterned tilework was unbelievably artistic, the colours from a palette of magic. Anna spent hours wandering and examining the treasures.

At her request Gazi would explain the significance of certain symbols, read and translate the beautiful calligraphic designs, so thoroughly she felt she was in a personal tutorial with a professional expert.

''How do you know so much about it?'' she asked him in amazement when he had described how certain tiles had been painted and fired, and he threw her a look.

''This is my people's culture and history and art,'' he said, in a voice like a cat's tongue on her skin. ''It is some of the greatest artistic and architectural achievement in the history of the human race. How should I not be familiar with it? Every Barakati is familiar with such things, as familiar as an English person with Shakespeare. But in addition it is my job to know such things.''

She was certainly learning more about her area of interest than she had ever learned at art college, and bit by bit she was packing in a wealth of inspiration that could probably carry her for years.

If only she didn't feel that she was also packing in future heartbreak.

* * *

"Something has to give," Anna muttered after several days of inaction.

Sheikh Gazi was on the phone trying to get through to the Barakati Embassy in London.

"Yes, today I will insist—why does no one answer?" Gazi said, exasperatedly listening to a recorded message. "It is noon in London, where is everyone? Ah, of course!" He lifted a hand. "Today is Friday, *juma,* they are all at the mosque." He put down the phone. "I will try again later."

"Friday?" she murmured, almost unable to believe that so much time had passed.

"The Friday prayer is the minimum required act of worship in the week. It is my own fault, I should have remembered."

He had certainly remembered earlier in the day, Anna thought absently. A bit before noon, he and the entire staff had left the house in a minivan, everyone dressed in their best. She and Safiyah had been left alone for an hour, and when the van returned only Gazi and the nurse were in it.

"Is that where you all went earlier? To the mosque?" Anna asked.

"Yes, all of my household who wish it have the right to be driven to the mosque for *juma*. It is far to walk. Then they go home to their families. Tonight you and I will eat at the hotel."

A little later Anna poured a subtle, spicy perfumed oil into her bath and afterwards dressed with care in a flowing, ivory silk *shalwar kamees* embroidered at breast and sleeve with deep blue thread and flat beads of lapis lazuli. Her tiny silver ear studs and silver rings were all the jewellery she had, but they at least suited the outfit. A gauzy navy stole and pair of navy leather thongs on her bare feet completed her outfit.

In the early evening she joined him at the front door, where a sports car was waiting. He drove them up the road to the Hotel Sheikh Daud for dinner in luxurious elegance on a balcony overlooking the sea. From here the view was much more open; she could see the whole stretch of the shoreline around the shallow bay, out into the water of the Gulf of Barakat.

Lights twinkled from the city, on the yachts out in the bay, and in the sprinkling of houses nestled in the forest along the shore. The sea and the sky were one deep, rich black, so that it seemed to her that the sky itself rushed onto the shore and retreated again, with that hypnotic roar and hiss.

A young woman sang haunting Barakati love songs, the food was deliciously cooked, and Gazi's eyes were on her almost constantly. Anna found herself floating away on a dream. A dream that was composed of Gazi's mouth, Gazi's eyes…

He watched her, knowing what she wanted. Her wide mouth stretching in a tremulous smile, her head tilting back to offer her slim throat, as if she knew how that posture in her excited him. His own mouth was tight with control.

"This song is so beautiful," she said dreamily, at the end of the meal, when their coffee cups were drained and the singer sang again. "Tell me what the words mean."

He unlocked his jaw. "They mean that a man is refusing to fall into a trap that a woman has set for him," he replied. "A woman he desires but does not trust. She dresses in beautiful jewels and robes, she perfumes her hair, she smiles, until he is driven mad with passion. But he cannot give in.''

In a brief pause in the music, his voice rasped on her ears, and Anna pressed her lips together. ''He can't?''

''He knows that she is forbidden to him.''

The music resumed on a haunting, wailing note, like a woman in the act of love. She made a little face of disappointment, and he thought that she would not look so if he made love to her.

''Why?'' Her eyes, inviting him, were dark as the night sky, her face beautiful as the moon.

''Because she is a cheat,'' Gazi said harshly.

The singer's voice joined the music again with a keening plaint. Fixed by his narrowed gaze, Anna could not turn away.

''So what happens?''

''He decides to make her admit her betrayal,'' Gazi said softly. ''He will pretend to love her, so that she will confess.''

''And he calls *her* a cheat?'' she asked.

''The song is about how the man fools himself as to his own motives. He is lying to himself. It is not for the reason he gives himself that he is going to make love to her, but because she has succeeded—before he even began.''

The music stopped, amid applause from the restaurant patrons.

''You are beautiful, Anna,'' he told her in a voice like gravel. ''You tempt me, with your soft looks, your willing mouth. I lie awake at night, wishing I were fool enough to believe that I could make love to you without danger. But it is not to be, Anna. You will not succeed.''

Eleven

———

At first, hearing the word *danger,* her heart thrilled, because she believed he meant that he was in danger of falling in love with her. But his voice and the expression in his eyes were so hard…and suddenly she understood.

She drew back into her chair, her brain sharp with suspicion. ''My God, you still think—!'' Suddenly it all fell into place. ''I've been here a *week* now, waiting for someone to perform a simple errand that Lisbet could have done in an hour! You've been delaying deliberately! What is going on?''

"I thought this way would be easier," he said, but she knew it was a lie.

"Easier for you!" she stormed. "Easier for you to keep me here against my will. Did you call back the embassy today, when the staff returned from the mosque?"

Gazi slapped a hand to his head. "Ah! I forgot!" He lifted his wrist and glanced at his watch. "Too late now. It is past seven o'clock in London."

"You forgot. And today's Friday, and I suppose the Barakati Embassy in London closes over the weekend?"

"All embassies in London, I believe, do so. I am sorry, Anna."

Anxiety choked her. Most of a week had gone by. He had manipulated her into doing exactly what he wanted, and fool that she was, she had spent the time dreaming.

"Is there a British Embassy in Barakat al Barakat?" she demanded.

"But of course!" he assured her blandly. "The British have always been on excellent diplomatic terms with Barakat, even though they never conquered us. The embassy is in Queen Halimah Square.''

''If my passport isn't here by Monday, I want to go to the embassy and ask them to issue me a temporary travel document so I can go home,'' Anna told him sternly.

''Very wise,'' he said, nodding. ''Yes, an excellent solution.''

''I want to stay here in the hotel tonight,'' she said.

He shrugged. ''As you wish. Will you go now and check in?''

Anna half got to her feet. ''Yes, I—'' She stopped, one hand on the back of her chair, and a nearby waiter came to her aid. She stood up because she had to, but stayed looking down at Gazi al Hamzeh. ''I don't have a credit card or anything.''

''Perhaps if you explain your situation, they will give you credit. Foreigners need passports to register in hotels here, but I am sure you can convince them to wait until you can apply to your embassy on Monday.''

Before she could come to any decision he was on his feet beside her, and the maître d' was hurrying over to bow his distinguished guest out.

Anna had always believed she had her fair share of courage. But she could not summon enough to make a stand now. The thought of trying to make herself understood, in a foreign language, a foreign country, while making a charge of abduction against a leading citizen— a Cup Companion of the ruling prince! And Gazi, as if knowing exactly what she was trying to get the courage for, remained deep in friendly conversation with the man, all the way to the door.

And only she knew, and he knew, that the dark expression in his eyes as he smiled at her was the look of a watchdog guarding a criminal.

They did not speak on the drive back to his house. Anna went straight to her own room, without a word.

She spent a restless night. Only the fact that, thanks to the tabloids, half the world knew where she was kept her from complete panic. She tossed and turned and looked back over the week and realized how easy a mark she had been. Time had slipped by, with sun and food and good talk…. He had her exactly where he wanted her. He had accused her of trying to tempt him. But it was Gazi who had been using constant temptation to keep her brain muddled.

How easily manipulated she had been by his interest in her! He had let her talk and talk. *It's a known brainwashing technique!* she reminded herself disgustedly. *It's what cults do with their marks—give them massive doses of attention. Love-bombing.* And even knowing that, how easily she had fallen for it.

And his Arab incompetence, his lack of appreciation of Western ideas of time—she began to blush for how easily she had fallen for the stereotype. Of course he had been faking all that. She had never met a man with a more incisive, better-informed mind. He spoke at least three languages! What could have possessed her to fall into the trap of believing that he could be so inefficient and ineffectual, could lack a basic understanding of Western culture?

She saw now that he had begun this act only

after she refused his invitation. He had deliberately become a caricature Arab. Anna snorted. It must have taken an extremely efficient organization to effect the abduction of her and the baby. That was a plan he had certainly conceived on his feet, and it had been flawlessly executed. From the time he found her in the hospital to the time the plane took off scarcely two hours had elapsed.

Clearly he had a crack team. Yet somehow he had fooled her into believing he couldn't organize getting her *handbag* from the very hospital he had abducted her and the baby from!

And still she had no idea why. What did he want from her? Why did he continue to think she was engaged in some kind of dishonesty? And above all, what was his reason for wanting to keep her here?

"Fly with me!"

"Willingly would I fly with thee, Beloved. But where can we fly, that is not ruled by your father or my prince?"

"India," she breathed.

He smiled at her, knowing she knew nothing save the name. "India is far, very far."

"For you I would suffer any hardship!" she cried.

"Beloved, if they catch us before we reach India, they will not let us live."

She smiled. "Choose fleet steeds, then, my Lion!"

He stood gazing out over the far horizon. "And if I say, stay here and live thy life as thy destiny demands—"

"I will fling myself from this parapet tomorrow night rather than wed him."

He turned and caught her to his chest, and stared into her eyes, his love a torment, because he was destined never to enjoy her beauty. But he could not tell her so. He put his lips on hers and tasted their deaths.

"Why then, we will fly to India," he said.

The dreams were profoundly disturbing, though she never quite remembered them. She would awaken suffocating with love and anguish, her heartbeat pounding through her system, yearning for him so desperately she could almost feel her dream lover beside her, as if his arms had only now let her go.

Her dream lover was Gazi al Hamzeh. And the dream seemed another reality, one that she half watched, half lived...always yearned for.

"I have had a phone call," Gazi said at breakfast. "Your passport has been picked up from your apartment. Today, if you wish, you can fly back to London. I will arrange for someone to meet you at the Immigration desk at Stansted airport with your passport."

She looked at him, one eyebrow raised. "If I wish? Of course I wish."

"You are determined to return?" he said softly. They were at a table on the balcony, looking out over the sun-kissed courtyard in the cool of the morning.

"Has not my home seemed to you like a good place to recuperate from your accident and restore yourself after your sorrows?" he asked, gesturing out to the paradise below them.

"In case you haven't noticed, I've had a week of that," she said. All her hackles were rising as she scented danger. Did he mean to prevent her again?

Gazi took another sip of the perfectly brewed coffee, set the cup in the saucer, and with an almost invisible flicker of his eyes, dismissed the attentive serving man, who nodded and slipped away.

''Anna, I would like to tell you…to explain something to you.''

''With a view to changing my mind about leaving?''

He hesitated. ''Perhaps. No—not necessarily. But in hopes that what you learn may change your mind about other things that you might plan to say or do.''

''Such as talk to the media.''

''And other things.''

Anna was curious, but she hesitated. ''Suppose you tell me what you want to tell me and it turns out you don't change my mind about anything at all?''

Gazi shrugged. ''Then of course you will do whatever suits you.''

She wondered if that was the truth. He had already kept her here a week against her will.

What new ploy might he come up with? But, she reflected, at least she would know more about why. That had to be an advantage.

"Fire away," she said, with a casualness she was far from feeling.

"Nadia, my sister, the mother of Safiyah, is missing. This you know. We are very worried about her."

"Who is 'we'?"

"I and my family. If you permit, I will tell you Nadia's story from the beginning," he said, and waited for her nod before beginning. "Three years ago, my father announced that he had chosen a husband for my sister. None of us knew until that moment that he was even considering such a step. It was an even greater surprise when we learned that he had chosen a man named Yusuf Abd ad Darogh. This was not a man my sister had any admiration for. She begged my father to go no further in it."

"Oh," she murmured.

"I tried to reason with my father." Anna picked up the echo of frustration and sorrow in his voice and tried to stop her heart softening towards him. "But my father was of the old school. In spite of all that we said, in spite of her deep unhappiness, Nadia was married to Yusuf.''

He gazed down at his coffee cup, which his hand absently clasped in a strong, loose embrace. Following the direction of his abstracted gaze, Anna had to close her own eyes. Something in the incipient power of the hold made her want to feel it close around her arm, her body....

''Yusuf's job then took him to the West,'' he was saying as she surfaced. ''He works for a large Barakati company, and he and Nadia moved to London. I am in London frequently, and of course I visited or spoke to Nadia on each visit. One of my brothers also.

''For the first year or so, things were apparently not intolerable. Then time went by, and Nadia did not become pregnant. She was becoming more and more anxious about it. We suspected that Yusuf was blaming her for it.''

Anna was listening now with her mouth soft, her eyes fixed on him, her sympathies entirely with Nadia. She heard an anxiety in his tone that proved that he loved his sister, and she couldn't help wanting to help him.

"Then at last Nadia became pregnant. But it made Yusuf no happier. It became difficult for us to get any reading on how Nadia was. More and more there was some excuse why visits were not convenient just at the moment, or she could not come to the phone. When we did visit we somehow were never allowed time with Nadia alone. And we gradually came to understand that she was only allowed to speak to any member of her family on the phone when Yusuf was in the room with her."

Anna shivered. "She must have felt totally helpless," she said.

"I am sure you are right, but if so, she was never able to express it."

He paused and cleared his throat. "My father died. When they returned to Barakat for the funeral, Nadia was wearing *hejab*. Here in Barakat even a simple headscarf is not worn outside of the mosque except by the religious old women. Nadia was wearing full black robe and scarf, no lock of hair showing, which is extreme by Barakati standards, and nothing

she herself would have wished. It is certain
that she was made to do it by Yusuf.

''Shortly after this, when they returned to
England, Nadia became ill with the pregnancy.
Too ill to speak to us when we phoned. Or
there were other excuses.''

Gazi paused, and an expression of self-
reproach tightened his mouth for a moment.
''There was a great deal to see to about my
father's estate. I was here in West Barakat virtually full-time for weeks. One day my brother
and I realized that neither of us had been allowed to speak to Nadia for almost two
months.''

Anna was listening too hard to be capable
of making a sound.

''We knew it was fruitless to try to phone
again. Yusuf would only put us off. My
brother and I flew in together on Friday last
week and arrived unannounced at their apartment. We found—we found Yusuf running
around the streets like a wounded animal,
screaming for Nadia and saying that she had
disappeared.

''He said that she had gone into labour

shortly before our arrival, and he had gone out to the garage—it is in a mews behind the house—for the car. When he drew up at the front door, it was open and Nadia was gone. That is what he said.''

Anna bit her lip. ''Was it—do you think he was lying?'' she whispered.

''There is no way to be sure,'' Gazi replied. ''It is possible he had warning that we were on our way and staged a show for our benefit. What reason could Nadia have for running away at such a time? She would want to go to the hospital to have her baby safely.''

''You don't think she was desperate and it was maybe—her only chance to escape?'' Anna offered quietly.

At this, Gazi bent forward, his hands clasped between his knees. ''Perhaps it is so, Anna, perhaps it is so. But now do you see how important your involvement is? You are the only lead we have. The question we must ask is, how did you come to be in a taxi with Nadia's baby? The answer to this may tell us much.''

She gazed at him, feeling how strong the

pull was. He had half hypnotized her, made her want to declare she was on his side. It was like pulling a tooth to stand up and walk away, out of his potent orbit. But she needed to think clearly, and she couldn't sitting so close to him. She had to do it.

Moving a little distance from the table towards an archway covered with greenery, she turned and said, "Well, thank you for telling me that. But it's *still* not the whole story, is it?"

"Why do you think so?" asked Sheikh Gazi. His gaze was just slightly wary, but she noted the change, and it proved her right.

She lifted her hands. "Because it's got more holes than a sponge! Excuse me, but there you are out combing the streets for your pregnant sister, and you just happen to search the casualty ward of the Royal Embankment Hospital, is that what I hear?"

He was watching her with steady disapproval. "There was an item on the radio that made me think I would find Nadia and her baby there. Instead I found you."

"On the radio?" she demanded disbelievingly.

"Yes, Anna," he said, and she was glad to
make him understand how it felt to have his
word doubted. "A silly item, meant to be
amusing—'mother, baby *and* cab driver all in
hospital and doing well.'"

"Ah! Okay, you found me. And you found
a baby you were instantly convinced was Nadia's. And what do you do? Do you call the
police and tell them your suspicions? Do you
claim the baby and take it home to Papa? No,
strangely enough, you *kidnap* me and this infant you are convinced is your niece, and you
immediately cart us off to Barakat! Now, that
needs a little more explaining than the current
version of your story offers. Because even a
man with your influence and connections, it
seems to me, and no doubt they reach to the
very top, isn't going to risk breaking the laws
of two countries without a very substantial reason.

"Unless, of course, your contempt for
women runs so deep you forgot that Safiyah
and I had any human rights at all. You're quick

to condemn your brother-in-law for keeping your sister a prisoner, but have you noticed that you are at this moment doing exactly the same thing to me?''

She saw that he was angered by that. ''I do not keep you prisoner!'' he exploded.

''What do you call it?'' Anna cried. She suddenly doubted whether the best course after all was challenging him. Her safest alternative probably had been to pretend to go along with whatever he suggested and then, when his guard was down, make good her escape. But she was too late.

''Why don't you tell me the truth, Sheikh Gazi?''

''I have told you the truth, so far as it goes.'' His eyes were hard. ''Recollect that you have still offered no coherent account of how you came to be in possession of my sister's baby.''

''Recollect that you have offered no convincing proof that the baby *is* your sister's!''

''There can be no question of it. My brother remains in London, pursuing enquiries. If any woman had reported her child missing, he would have discovered it.''

"How do you know that some past girl-friend of your own hasn't given birth and abandoned the baby? Maybe I found her!"

"You are being ridiculous," he said, his face hard. "The baby was in a satchel that had obviously been prepared for a hospital mater-nity visit. In that satchel, which has now been picked up from the Royal Embankment Hos-pital, were items recognizably my sister's."

"All right, let's assume Safiyah is your sis-ter's baby, then. What do you suspect *me* of? Your little team has had the keys to my apart-ment for the best part of a week by now," she told Gazi coldly. "Don't you feel that if there was anything at all to connect me with your sister they'd have found it?"

Gazi took a breath, trying for calm. "Nev-ertheless, it is very difficult to imagine any sce-nario in which you are completely uninvolved. You must see that. What am I to guess? That the hospital mistakenly mixed up two casual-ties, leaving Nadia with no baby? That Safiyah was abandoned at the precise place where you had your accident?"

"As far as I'm concerned, either of those is

more likely than that I went out of my tiny mind and kidnapped a baby, all during the one half hour of my life that I don't happen to have any memory of.''

''All right.'' Gazi's full, usually generous mouth was drawn tight. ''I will tell you more. Nadia's husband, Yusuf, may suspect that the baby is not his. In Yusuf's mind his suspicion would be enough. In such a case, it is not easy to guess what he intended to do, but it is almost certain that he would not allow Nadia to keep the child and raise it as his own.''

She felt a little chill in the warm breeze, and shuddered.

''It was in the hopes of preventing Yusuf discovering that we had found Safiyah that we rushed her out of the country in the way we did. This would have succeeded, but for your actions. The press has created huge potential risk by running photos of me arriving in Barakat al Barakat with a baby. Yusuf of course now suspects that the child is Nadia's.''

His voice was hard with suspicion. Anna frowned and took a step back towards the table where he sat. ''You thought I deliberately showed the baby to the cameras to let Yusuf know you had her?''

He was sitting in a casual but not a relaxed posture, one elbow on the chair arm, his hand supporting his cheek. ''There seemed very little other excuse for such wanton disregard of the baby's safety.''

Anna gasped indignantly. ''I did it to protect the baby from *you*!'' she informed him hotly, flinging herself back into her chair. ''I didn't know the paparazzi were even there. You had convinced me the baby was ours, but you sure hadn't convinced me you had any affection for me! I thought you were going to try to snatch her! You told me nothing but lies! How was I supposed to guess what was going on?''

He raised an eyebrow, but did not comment, merely said, ''Fortunately the press blunted the damage by printing that the baby is ours, and even hinted that Safiyah is several weeks old.''

She laughed in irritation. How stupid did he think she was? ''Fortunately? You told them that, didn't you? You've already admitted that your job is in press relations, so you've got all the necessary contacts.''

He waited for her to finish and then went on. "It was of crucial importance in deflecting Yusuf's suspicions. Yusuf will believe what he sees in print if we reinforce it. Or at least, don't contradict it. That is why I hoped that you would agree to remain unavailable for a while. Not to deny the press stories."

"And when I refused, you forced my compliance through trickery."

"There are lives at stake," Sheikh Gazi said.

"Why the hell didn't you tell me there were lives at stake, then, instead of trying to bribe me with sun and fun and money and sex?"

"Sex?" he asked, his eyebrow up. "Do I try to bribe you with sex, or has that been the other way?"

Suddenly danger of a different sort whispered on the breeze. Anna snapped, "What reason could you possibly have for suspecting that I would want to bribe you with sex? What would I hope to achieve?"

"That is something only you know!" he bit out, his own anger flaring suddenly, making Anna jump. "I find you with my sister's baby, you can give no reasonable explanation, you deliberately show her to reporters after I have successfully smuggled her out of England—'' He broke off. ''Did you give me any reason to trust you? You threatened me with exposure for having abducted Safiyah! What—''

''I *never* threatened you! I told you I had no intention of exposing you! I said I would do nothing more than deny—''

They were by this time almost shouting.

''To go back to England and to deny that Safiyah is our child is to send Yusuf a notarized declaration that she is Nadia's daughter,'' Gazi said coldly. ''Now, if you are involved with Yusuf in any way, I ask you to tell me what your involvement is. And if you are not involved, I ask you to go on with the charade that has been created until we find the truth.

''For the love of God, Anna!'' he cried as she hesitated. ''My sister may be at this moment her husband's prisoner. Or hiding in some alley, snatching food from rubbish tins. Have you a heart, Anna, to appreciate what she may be suffering, and to help her?''

Twelve

She met him at the stables, in her disguise as a page, while the sounds of revelry still rose on the air from the palace. He dared use no light, nor kiss her, but only turned silently to lead her through dark, tortuous passages to the great city wall.

She climbed the rope ladder ahead of him, bravely, without a murmur of fear, and he thought what a wife she would have made him, if things had been otherwise.

On the other side, still without speech, he led her to the outcrop within which he had tethered two horses. With one quick embrace only, one whispered word of courage, he tossed her into the saddle.

They rode out towards the dawn.

They arrived in London at midmorning, and it was only when she felt the wheels touch down and saw the familiar landmarks that Anna started breathing again

She had agreed to return to London and make her arrangements as quietly as possible, to head straight to France and hide out at the villa of her clients without speaking to the media.

At Immigration, they were met as promised, by an escort of three bodyguards, one of whom handed over her passport. Sheikh Gazi, she noticed, was travelling on a Barakati diplomatic passport, and they were allowed to enter Great Britain with barely a nod. No one even questioned why or how she had left the country without a passport.

Then they came through the doors into the terminal and were faced with a crowd of excited paparazzi.

Anna stopped as if she had walked into a

wall. She could hear the noise of clicking cameras, but the shouted questions might as well have come from the Tower of Babel for all she could understand. She swayed.

"How on *earth* did they find out we were arriving?" she cried, astonished at the sheer numbers.

"Anna, Anna!" "Can you look this way?" "Smile for the folks, Anna!" "Are you happy? How's the baby, Anna?" "Did the baby come with you?" "What's your baby's name, Anna?"

Then a strong arm was around her, and Sheikh Gazi's hand was gripping her arm above the elbow, urging her forward. He leaned into her ear and murmured, "Walk quickly but on no account run. Let me handle them."

This was a command she was only too relieved to obey.

His voice was low and for her ear alone, and in spite of everything it raised yearning in her heart, and heat in her blood. "Look at me."

She looked nervously over her shoulder into his face, and met a glance of such lazy, sexy approval her stomach rolled over. Anna stumbled, and his strong embrace steadied her. She smiled involuntarily, her whole self stretching and basking in his unexpected admiration like a cat in a sunbeam.

The photographers cried out their satisfaction. "Kiss her, Gazi!" someone cried, and Anna's heart thumped. But the sheikh only laughed lightly and shook his head.

They moved quickly after that, his bodyguards doing no more than create a little breathing space as the group of journalists ran beside them through the terminal to the exit, calling questions.

"How do you feel about the baby, Sheikh Gazi?"

"What do you think, Arthur?" he called, as if it should be obvious.

"Did you get Prince Karim's approval?"

"He has never disapproved, to my knowledge."

"When's the wedding? Have you set the date?"

"No," the sheikh's deep voice responded above her ear.

"Are you going to?"

Sheikh Gazi threw the last questioner a smile. "Julia, you'll be the first to know."

Questions and answers were following each other in such a rapid-fire way it was a moment before Anna took it all in. She blinked and turned to him. "What are you—?" she began, but he put a warning grip on her arm.

"Let me handle it, Anna!" he said again.

It terrified her. He was doing it again. Forcing her into compliance through circumstance. She had not agreed to look the press in the eye and pretend it was true, and now she was frightened. Had he ever told her the truth? Was she a pawn in something she didn't know about? Suddenly she doubted the truth of everything he had said. He had a much deeper reason for this constant manipulation of her. He must.

Anna swallowed, coughed and forced herself to turn to the nearest man with a notebook.

"I am not Sheikh Gazi's mistress," she said.

"Great!" he said, scribbling. "Can I say fiancée?"

"No! Don't say I'm his fiancée! And the baby is not—"

"The baby is not with us!" Gazi cried over her, drowning her out. "The doctor thought it better."

His arm went tight around her and he was swooping her through the main exit to where a limousine waited by the curb, the rear door already open.

Anna threw one wild look along the half-deserted road. Wherever she ran now, she would be chased by all these journalists, and they would certainly catch up with her. What would she say then, what could she do? She could not simply deny that she was his mistress and that the baby was hers and then expect to disappear. They would hound her unmercifully for the whole story. And if she told it...Gazi had powerful friends.

Feeling like every kind of coward, Anna got into the limousine. Gazi quickly followed. One of the bodyguards got into the back with them, the other two in front with the driver, and a second later they were pulling away from the happy mob of journalists.

She turned to Sheikh Gazi al Hamzeh. "How did they know we were arriving?" she demanded furiously.

"In a moment," he said, then turned to the other man. "Anything?" he asked.

The man shook his head. He looked younger than the sheikh, and she thought she could detect a facial resemblance between them. "Still not a trace," he said. "She has evaporated into air, Gazi. Yusuf insists he knows nothing, and unless we're willing to show our hand with him, there's no saying if that's the truth or not."

He had none of the air of a man talking to his employer. As if in confirmation of this judgement, he turned suddenly to Anna. "Hi, Anna," he said, with an engaging smile. "I'm Jafar. People here call me Jaf."

"Hello," she said slowly. She glanced back and forth between the two men.

"Jafar is my brother," Sheikh Gazi said quietly.

"It's great of you to play along, Anna," said Jaf. "We really appreciate it."

Anna didn't return his smile. "Thank your

brother,'' she said. ''I had nothing to say about it.''

She seemed to herself not to start breathing again until the familiar sights of Chelsea met her eyes and she could believe that Gazi was going to do what he said and take her home.

There were a few journalists on the street in front of the ramshackle Victorian house where she had an apartment, and as the three went up the walk there were more shouted questions.

Anna left it to Gazi to talk to them, already rooting for her keys in the little shoulder bag Jaf had given back to her at the airport. But no key chain met her searching fingers. Anna clicked her tongue and lifted the bag to eye level, just as Gazi produced her keys and unlocked the door.

So Jaf had passed over her keys to Gazi instead of herself.

They all moved inside the small front hall and closed the outer door on the paparazzi. Then she held out her hand and said sharply, ''My keys, please.''

She waited, staring at him, until Gazi put her keys in her hand. A moment later she stepped through her own door, followed by Jaf and Sheikh Gazi, and led the way upstairs.

The phone was ringing. Anna moved into the main room as the answering machine picked up. She stood looking around her for a moment, trying to orient herself in her own life.

The room was long, with windows at each end. The south-facing half, overlooking the street, was her sitting room, with a fireplace, sofa and chairs; the north, whose windows overlooked an overgrown courtyard with a tree, was her studio, with trestle tables, trolleys, rolls of paper, a couple of painted screens that she was working on for a client. Two broad expanses of wall down both sides of the room were covered with sketches, paintings, photos, colour swatches and other bits and pieces of her working life.

Underneath them, painted on the plaster, was a series of arches not unlike those she had seen for real in Gazi's house. Anna blinked and wondered if it was merely her own mural that had given her the idea she was at home there.

It just did not feel like only a week since she had dressed for her meal with Cecile and Lisbet. She felt strange, removed from her old life, as if she hadn't been here for months.

"Hello, Anna. This is Gabriel DaSouza from the *Sun*...."

She mentally shut out the voice coming from the answerphone, and moved towards the sofa. On the table in front of it was spread the week's mail, including a few scribbled notes from the press.

Anna frowned, wondering who had placed them there, and just then heard a step in the kitchen. She whirled, her heart jumping into her throat.

"Hi!" said Lisbet. "I made the coffee while I was waiting. Jaf figured we'd all need it."

Lisbet kicked off her shoes and under Jaf's interested gaze slid her long, black-stockinged legs behind Anna on the sofa as she accepted the cup of coffee Anna had poured for her.

"Frankly, it's a mystery to me, too," she told Anna. "You ask what happened—absolutely nothing. Someone pulled up in a cab and got out, you got in. The cab drove off. It took Ceil and me a couple of minutes to flag another one. Ceil dropped me at home. That was all I knew until someone phoned me at sparrow's peep Sunday morning to say was that Anna Lamb in this morning's *Sun?* I said it couldn't possibly be you. And then Alan said you'd called him...."

Jaf leaned forward, taking his own cup from Anna's hand. "Someone got out of the cab, you say. Did you notice who?"

Lisbet pursed her lips and shook her head. "It was on the other side of the street and I wasn't really paying attention."

"Try to think back. You may have seen something. One person, a couple?"

Lisbet obligingly closed her eyes and tried to visualize the scene. "There was a tree just there—someone came past it, but whether that was whoever got out of the cab or not...one person, I think. Dressed in black, maybe, with street lighting it's—wait! There was someone in black a couple of minutes later, too. I wonder if it was the same person? By the bridge."

Lisbet opened her eyes. "I noticed her because she seemed to be wearing one of those black things that cover a woman from head to foot and I thought it was strange to see a Muslim woman by herself there at night.''

''Battersea Bridge?'' Jaf prompted.

Lisbet nodded. ''Yes, the Riverfront isn't far from there, and we were sort of strolling in that direction after Anna left, looking for a cab. This woman crossed the road ahead of us and went onto the bridge. But I don't know that she was the person who got out of the cab Anna caught. There was something about her that drew my eye, I can't really say what it was.''

Anna, meanwhile, put her hands up to her face. A woman in black. She smelled the scent of the river at night, autumn leaves.... She dropped her hands again and found Sheikh Gazi's eyes on her.

''What have you remembered?'' he asked softly.

She shook her head sadly. ''Nothing.''

They sat drinking coffee without speaking for several minutes. Lisbet was lost in thought. She surfaced and said, ''Unless something completely weird and incredibly unlikely happened after you got into that cab, Anna, the accident must have happened within a couple of minutes. He turned the corner, drove straight along Oakley to the King's Road and smashed into the bus. Five minutes max.''

''That's what I think.''

''So either someone walked up to the accident scene and slipped the baby into the crashed cab knowing that an ambulance would be coming, which, let's face it, is pretty far-fetched, or…or you got into a cab with a baby already in it.''

''Yes.'' Anna nodded.

''Or else some completely off-the-wall thing happened in the hospital.''

As her friend put into words just what she herself had been trying to say to Sheikh Gazi, Anna felt what a huge relief it was to have her integrity reaffirmed after his suspicions. She glanced at him to see how he was taking this, but his face gave nothing away.

Lisbet went on, ''So putting myself in Nadia's place…I'm running away from an abusive husband, but I'm already in labour, right?

So I—what? Give birth in the back of a cab? But then the driver would have radioed an emergency call to get an ambulance to the scene, wouldn't he? Was there such a call?''

''No,'' said Jaf, sitting forward. Lisbet was certainly convincing while she was getting into a part.

''Or he would get her straight to a hospital. What he *wouldn't* do is pull up on the Embankment and drop his passenger, with or without her baby. So, let's assume for the moment that Nadia was the person who got out of the cab that you got into, Anna, and that she left the baby in it. Doesn't it follow that she had already given birth, and *then* flagged the cab to take her somewhere?''

''Yes...'' Anna said slowly, the excitement of discovery building in her. This was starting to feel right.

Jaf said, ''The baby was absolutely newborn, wrapped in a woman's bathrobe and laid inside a satchel. She had not been washed. The hospital guessed that the driver had stopped to assist in the birth and then had hastily wrapped the baby and resumed the journey to the hospital, when the accident occurred. He is still not able to be questioned.''

Anna glanced at Gazi. ''She might have given birth in the apartment, and when he went for the car, she just ran out into the streets.''

Lisbet pursed her lips.

''You and your brother were both out of town, right? Who in London could Nadia go to, with her baby? Who could she trust not to call her husband?''

Jaf shook his head. ''She had no childhood friends in London, only those she had met since moving here three years ago. And we think her social life was very restricted.''

''So maybe something like a women's shelter would have been her only option. Was she on her way to one? Have you checked whether there are any shelters in the neighbourhood of Battersea Bridge?''

Jaf smiled. ''We have not before thought about concentrating on this area, of course. I will see what can be done, but women's shelters are very secretive.''

''The big question is, what changed Nadia's mind? Why did she leave the baby in the cab?

If she *was* going to a shelter, surely…'' Lisbet faded off thoughtfully.

Sheikh Gazi intervened at last. ''That is the flaw in an otherwise excellent argument. If she went to a women's shelter, why not take the baby with her? And in addition, whether she went to such a place, or to friends we know nothing about, why has she not called us?''

Lisbet hesitated. ''I hate to—uh.'' She glanced at Anna for guidance. Anna, catching her meaning, shrugged.

Lisbet turned to Gazi. ''I have one advantage over you here. I *know* that Anna isn't involved in the way you suspect. I know that she doesn't know any guy named Yusuf, and that she wouldn't be involved in anything like baby-snatching if she did,'' she said firmly, and Anna suddenly felt like crying. ''I also know that if she says she was confused after the accident and has amnesia about a critical moment, that's the exact truth. So.''

She heaved a breath. No one else spoke. ''I don't want to distress you, and please forgive me if this suggestion is way off beam, but is it possible that...I mean, unhappy people have been known to...do you think Nadia went to the bridge because jumping seemed the only way out?''

Thirteen

———

"**I**'ve got to go," Lisbet said, looking at her watch a few minutes later. "We've got a night shoot up on Hampstead Heath tonight and I'm due in Makeup in an hour." She turned to Anna. "Do you want to come and hang out for a while?"

The question was put casually, but Anna knew that it was her friend's way of extricating her from a difficult situation. If she went with Lisbet, Sheikh Gazi and his brother would have no option but to leave.

But she found herself shaking her head.

"I've got to get to France, Lisbet. I'm only half packed and I have to organize my ticket."

Lisbet lifted an eyebrow as if she understood more than Anna was confessing. "Well, phone me on my mobile later. I'll probably be hanging around doing nothing most of the night."

"All right."

Lisbet slipped into her shoes and a smart little jacket, put sunglasses on her nose.

"Would you allow me to take you where you have to go?" Jaf offered, and Lisbet's mouth was pulled in an involuntary, slow smile.

"Sure," she said easily.

"They will photograph us," Jaf warned, gesturing towards the windows and the photographers still waiting in the street below. "Do you mind?"

Lisbet laughed. "I'm an actress, Jaf. Publicity is everything."

A moment later Gazi and Anna watched from the windows as Lisbet and Jaf braved the journalists and slipped into the back of the limo. As the limo pulled away she turned to look at him, and all at once the silence weighed very heavily in the room.

"Well," Anna said. "Sorry we couldn't be more help."

Sheikh Gazi took her hand, but not in a handshake, and stared into her eyes. "You can be of more help," he said, in a rough, urgent voice. She felt a surge of energy from him travel up her arm to her throat and chest.

"I really—" Anna coughed to clear her throat. "I really can't, you know, unless I remember something. But I do think Lisbet's right. The baby had to be in the cab when I got into it."

"That is not what I mean, Anna."

Her heart began a wild dance in her breast. She stared at him, licked her lip unconsciously and, taking her hand from his, turned away to hide the heat she felt burning up in her cheeks.

He was mesmerizing, he really was. He had the most extraordinary ability to turn himself off and on. A few minutes ago, listening to Lisbet, he had gone to low voltage, Anna thought wildly, effacing himself in some mysterious way to watch and listen. Now he was high-powered again.

"I'm almost afraid to ask," she joked, nervous of her own deep response.

He looked at her with a frown and turned her towards him, his eyes searching her face till she felt exposed and vulnerable, was trembling. She had never felt so emotionally fragile just at a man's look. Almost shaking with nerves, she lifted her hands up and placed them against his chest. She felt his body react to the jolt of the connection, and his eyes darkened suddenly, like a cat's.

And then his arms were around her, and he was staring down into her upturned face. "Anna," he murmured, his lips inches from her own. She felt him tremble and with fainting pleasure recognized in him a mixed desire to cherish her and yet crush her against himself.

Then he closed his eyes, and she felt him tense with a huge effort of will. In the next moment she was released. He dropped his arms and stepped back.

"We must talk," he said.

A little laugh of bitter disappointment escaped her. So she was still the woman who was a cheat, whose temptation he must resist.

"Must we?"

"Anna, what your friend said has changed the picture. You must see this."

"Yes, and how does it affect me?" she asked, blowing air out hard and turning away as she tried to get a grip on the passionate ache her arms felt to hold him.

"It is no longer enough, Anna, that you agree simply to disappear to France and say nothing to the press."

She turned to look over her shoulder at him with deep hostility. "Why not?" she demanded.

"They are out there, Anna. They know you now—they will chase you for the story."

"And whose fault is that? Are you suggesting it was *not* your brother who notified everyone and his dog of our arrival time?"

"No, you are right. It was Jaf who did this. I am sorry. We thought only to take one last advantage of your presence, to get one more story that might convince Yusuf. But now things are more desperate.''

''But Lisbet didn't tell you anything you didn't already know—or guess.''

''Yes,'' he contradicted. ''May we sit down again?''

It was a command, and her reaction was to turn towards a chair. A sudden draft made her feel how the temperature was dropping outside—or perhaps it was inside her own heart—and Anna stooped and flicked on the gas fire in the fireplace before flinging herself into an armchair on one side of it.

The gas ignited with a whoosh. Sheikh Gazi took the chair opposite her, on the other side of the fireplace. Then for a moment he turned his gaze to blink thoughtfully at the flames leaping up around the fake coal.

She watched him. The bone structure of his face was emphasized by the firelight flickering over it in the gathering dusk, revealing sensitivity at temple and mouth. In this light he looked like an old portrait of a saint, sensuous and ascetic together. She suddenly saw, behind the playboy handsomeness, that he was a man used to the rigours of self-discipline. And he was exerting it now.

Sheikh Gazi stared into the fire. He began speaking slowly. "Ramiz Bahrami has been my close friend most of my life. His family is from one of the ancient tribes in the mountains of Noor, but his father moved to the capital to serve the old king. Ramiz and I went to school in the palace and later to university together. He is a close, personal friend of Prince Karim. Highly trusted."

Anna blinked, her lips parting in surprise, and he flicked his eyes from the fire to her face. She saw open pain in them, and her heart hurt for him.

"My sister Nadia and Ramiz fell in love. She could not have chosen a better man. It was when Ramiz approached my father to ask for permission to marry Nadia that we were all rocked by the information that my father had already chosen Yusuf for her.

"I told you I argued with my father. I tell you now I never pleaded so strongly with him about anything before or since. But he would not give in. Ramiz was a university-educated, moderate Muslim with political ambitions, and Yusuf was mosque-educated, ignorant of the world, devout. It was one thing for my father to let his sons be educated at university. It was another thing entirely to give his daughter to such a man.''

He was silent for a moment, staring into the flames.

''How did Ramiz react to his refusal?'' she prompted softly.

''They both took it hard. Very hard. Ramiz appealed to the prince to intervene, but although Prince Karim did make a request, he knew very well that a father cannot be ordered even by a prince in such a matter.

''Ramiz wanted to run away with her. I would have assisted them, but Nadia was raised with a strong sense of religious duty. She felt it right to obey my father, even in this. And she knew that such a thing in any case would ruin Ramiz's political career.''

He breathed. ''She said no. I was sorry for it, and yet I knew she was right.''

If he was trying to get her onside with this

recital, he was succeeding. Anna's heart was deeply touched.

"Ramiz left the country before the wedding—Prince Karim kindly sent him on some mission abroad. He did not return until Yusuf and Nadia had come here to London."

"Has Ramiz married?" Anna asked softly.

He looked at her, shaking his head once. "No. He devoted himself to work. Karim trusts him absolutely. For the past year he has been engaged on something that took him to various countries. For a while he was in Canada.

"It is only since Nadia's disappearance that I have learned from the prince that Ramiz spent part of the past year here in London."

She gasped. "Do you think they met?"

"Now that the pieces come together a little, I begin to believe that they met. I think that this was the root of Yusuf's jealousy, of his suspicion that Nadia's baby was not his own."

"Did Yusuf know that Ramiz and Nadia were in love?"

"It is possible that my father confided something to Yusuf. I cannot say it is not so. My father might have hoped in this way to prevent trouble by alerting Yusuf to the danger.''

She could say nothing. What a wholesale betrayal of a daughter.

Gazi took a breath. ''Anna, the story is not over. Ramiz disappeared several months ago, and Prince Karim cannot be certain where he was at the time of his disappearance. But it is very possible that he was in England.''

''Are you...are you saying Yusuf killed him?''

Again pain was mirrored on his face. ''We can't be certain. Ramiz may even be alive. But it seems more of a possibility now that Ramiz's disappearance, rather than being connected with his secret work for Prince Karim, was because of his personal life.''

''Do you think that Yusuf is right? Is Safiyah Ramiz's baby and not his own?''

''How can I be certain unless we have tests done? It will be some time before this can be arranged. And time is something we do not have.

''Anna, if your friend is right, and it was Nadia she saw that night...if Nadia is dead and

Ramiz also, then it is possible that Safiyah is the only heir either of them will ever have.

"As things stand, as the legal father under English law, Yusuf has the right to custody of Safiyah. I cannot give up custody of the only child my sister and my friend will ever have to such a man as this, and with such a motive to hate her.

"Anna, I ask you, as a woman who knows the value of one child's life, to go on with the pretence we have started. Let the world think we are lovers. Pretend Safiyah is our child. Stay with me until we have discovered the fate of Nadia and Ramiz."

He wasted no time acting on her capitulation. By the time she had hastily thrown a few things into a bag, completed her half-made arrangements for leaving the flat unoccupied for a few weeks, and written a note for the downstairs tenant, another limousine was waiting to sweep them off to London's most prestigious hotel.

There they went to a huge suite on the top floor, with wonderful views overlooking Hyde

Park. "We must give the press as much fodder as we can," he told her. "The more Yusuf reads about us in the papers, the more he will believe."

Before anything else, Gazi insisted that Anna should be examined by another medical expert on head injury. The surgeon, who seemed to be a personal friend, however, was as cheerful as his counterpart in Barakat had been.

"It's not uncommon for accident victims to experience amnesia such as yours," he reassured Anna. "The period of time immediately surrounding the trauma is lost. In fact, it's unlikely you'll ever regain those minutes. But there is absolutely nothing to worry about."

After that she went to the private Health Suite, where she had a steam bath and a massage, and emerged feeling totally pampered. Then she went downstairs to see a top hairdresser, and then a makeup artist.

She returned to the suite to find that several outfits had been sent up from a boutique downstairs for her choice.

"Choose something for tonight," Gazi ordered her. "We will have dinner in a club. Tomorrow we will go shopping in the stores."

She chose a simply cut, utterly luxurious full-length coat and spaghetti-strap dress in black velvet. She had never worn anything so expensive in her life. The outfit clung to her, emphasizing her fashionable thinness.

She emerged from her bedroom, feeling she had never looked so stylish in her life, to find Gazi at a desk in the sitting room of the suite. He looked up, and for an instant his eyes burned her. Then he dropped his eyes and snapped open one of several cases on the desk.

"Diamonds, perhaps," he said with forced casualness, offering it to her.

Anna gasped when she looked inside. "Oh, goodness, where did these come from?"

He raised an eyebrow. "From the jeweller downstairs." He lifted from its silky bed a fabulous necklace that seemed to burn with cold fire, and when he slipped it around her neck she was almost surprised that it didn't scorch her skin. "Do you like diamonds, Anna?"

She laughed, delighted at the utter madness of her life, and turned to the mirror above the fireplace. "I've never really been on speaking terms with diamonds," she said. "But I'm quite happy to wear a necklace like this tonight, I promise you!"

Later, sitting at the table beside her on an intimately small, semicircular bench seat in a place so famous Anna had to pinch herself to believe it, Gazi observed, "Diamonds are too cold for you. You should wear coloured stones. Sapphires, to match your eyes."

Anna only laughed, shaking her head, and fingered one of the earrings.

"You must wear a variety of jewels over the next day or so," he said. "Then, it will please me if you will choose the set you like best to keep. As a gift of gratitude."

Anna almost choked on the tiny garlic mushroom she was eating as a starter. "Choose a *set* of jewels?" she exclaimed, putting a hand to her throat, and feeling the diamonds glowing there. "You're joking! These must be worth a fortune!"

"What you are doing for Nadia is worth much more to me," Gazi said.

Anna gazed down at the beautiful diamonds encircling her wrist, shaking her head. ''Thank you. Not that I have anything against jewellery, Sheikh Gazi, but there's something else that I'd much rather have.'' She looked up. ''It would be a real favour, if you—''

His face darkened with an unreadable expression. His gaze raked her with an intensity that held more fire than the diamonds, leaving her gasping for air. Anna breathed and thought, *God, he thinks I'm going to ask him to make love to me*— But before the thought was completed, the sheikh was in control of himself again.

''Whatever you ask for, if I can,'' he said levelly.

She could hardly speak, for the thought of what that unguarded moment had told her was choking her. Desire pulled at her, drew her lips into a trembling smile. She could not control that, for what else could his look mean, but that he wanted her, and for some reason known to himself, was exercising rigid control?

In the moment when that control had slipped, she had felt a powerful passion ema-

nating from him. Her whole body seemed to
be made of butterflies now, all fluttering, so
that nothing but thought held her being together. She was so fragile she would dissolve
in the smallest gust of wind.

She knew that he could not remain in control if she challenged him. The thought was
like champagne to her system, making her
drunk.

She swallowed and tried to speak.

"Tell me," he commanded, and Anna struggled to bring her own thoughts back in line.

"I just—it just occurred to me that you
could maybe mention to people that I'm a mural artist, specializing in Middle Eastern
themes. It would be such fabulous publicity for
me. And if as a result I got even one commission from—" she lifted a hand and gestured
around the room, where more than one table
had recognizable faces "—from someone like
this, well, I'd be muralist to the stars, wouldn't
I?"

He stared at her, his eyes narrowed. "And
you would rather have this than precious
stones?"

Anna smiled, biting her lip. "It would be a lot more useful over the long term."

"You are a very unusual woman."

Jealousy clawed her, and she didn't think before she spoke. "But then I suppose the favours I'm providing are a little different than what you're used to, too."

His eyes went black as he got it, and his hand found hers on the table between them and crushed it as he stared into her eyes. All the breath left her body in one grunting moan at the suddenness of the change in him. She thought, *I've done it, he's lost control,* and the thought made her blood wild.

"It will not be a favour, Anna, from me or from you, when it happens," he growled between his teeth, and kissed her hand with a mouth drawn tight with passionate control. "It is a necessity between us. You know it."

She felt passion like burning heat in his touch, saw it in his eyes, felt it rush through her body so powerfully she was dimly grateful she was not standing. Gazi was trembling as his hand released hers and came up to stroke her temple, her cheek. She shivered.

"Is it not so? Do you not feel it so?"

She couldn't have said a word to save her life, she was so swamped with feeling. She tried to swallow, but her throat was choked.

"I have seen it in your eyes, Anna! In every move you make!" he insisted. "Do you deny it?"

She opened her mouth and dropped her head back, trying to catch her breath. Electric sensuality roared through her, setting every part of her alight.

"I have wanted you until I was mad," he whispered hoarsely. "Your perfume, your mouth, your body stretched out in the sun...what it cost me, hour after hour, day after day, to see you there, to feel how you wanted to tempt me—*ya Allah!* how I wanted you!"

"Gazi!" she whispered helplessly.

"And do you challenge me now with talk of favours? Favour?" His voice grated over her charged nerves, blinding her with sensation, making her faint. "Shall I ask you for this as a favour, and offer you jewels in return? How much will you ask, I wonder? A diamond for each kiss, Anna? Another for every thrust of my tongue into your sweet mouth, to make us both mad with wanting more? And what, to touch your breasts? A bracelet of sapphires?''

His voice dropped to a tiger's hungry growl. She could feel his breath against her neck. ''To open your legs for me, Anna, what for this favour? A necklace, a tiara? I give it to you, yes! If it were necessary I would bury you in jewels, make love to you on a bed of diamonds and rubies and then give them all to you.''

His eyes burned her, heat licking through her body, melting everything into wild need.

''But it will not be necessary, Anna—will it? Do you think I do not know that to make you open your legs I need only ask with my tongue for entry? If I press my kiss on you there, Anna, who does whom the favour? Tell me that you too do not want this, if you can. Tell me the thought of my tongue on your body is not part of your dreams as it is of mine.''

''Stop,'' she moaned helplessly. ''My God, Gazi, stop, I'm—''

''Think of opening your legs to my kiss,

Anna," he commanded, watching how desire burned her and made her tremble, devouring her need. "Think of my tongue, my mouth, think how the heat will stir you, make you need what only I can give you. How you will cry out, and beg for more."

"Gazi," she pleaded. "Gazi, I can't take it."

"Yes," he said, deliberately misunderstanding her. "Yes, you can take more than this. You must. Do you think I can stop there? No, once we start, Anna—"

He lifted her hand to his mouth again, and bit the fleshy part of her palm between strong white teeth. A thousand nerves leapt into wildest reaction, and she could scarcely stifle the moan that rose to her throat.

"What comes next, Anna? Who will beg whom for the favour of my body inside you, hmm? Will we not beg each other for it? Say it!" he commanded.

She wondered dimly how she would survive. She opened her eyes and mouth at him, struggling for control.

"Tell me!" he commanded again.

She licked her dry lips, opened her mouth for air. "Tell you what?"

"Tell me whether you will ask me for the favour, Anna. Tell me that you will want it, too. Or will it be a favour you grant me when I ask?"

Feeling coursed up and down her body, through every cell.

She dropped her head. "You know I want you," she said, scarcely getting the words out.

It was as if she struck him with all her strength. She saw his back straighten with a jolt, his head turn to one side. His eyes never left hers, and she saw blackness like the centre of a storm, and realized that he had, at last, been driven beyond his strength.

Fourteen

———

It was at that moment that their lobsters arrived. She saw Gazi flick an unbelieving glance at the waiter, and at the plate, saw his hand clench. Then his eyes moved from the deliciously steaming lobster slowly up to her face, and he smiled a smile that sent little rivulets of sensation all over her.

They were silent as the pepper grinder made its ritual pass over both plates and then Gazi picked up a claw of the lobster between his strong fingers. His hands clenched till the knuckles showed white, and she quivered where she sat, knowing it was a sign not of exertion, but control. The shell broke open to reveal the tender white meat.

His hand not quite steady, he dipped the triangular wedge of flesh in butter, lifted it and held it out invitingly to her mouth. Anna tried to speak, failed, licked her lips and then submitted, leaning forward a little to take the meat between her teeth and pull it delicately from the shell.

He watched her chew and lick the butter from her mouth, with a smile that took her breath away. She dropped her eyes to her own plate, picked up the cracker and broke a piece of shell, then did as he had done, dipping the tender juicy flesh into butter, and holding it for him to eat.

When his teeth closed firmly on the meat, biting it, drawing it out, and then eating it with sudden, uncontrolled hunger, a shaft of purely sexual sensation went through her. Anna grunted, and his eyelids flickered.

The meal that followed was torment, the torment of overcharged senses. Anna had never experienced a sensuality to equal it in all her life. They fed themselves and each other without plan, with their bare hands, with forks, biting, chewing, licking, and fainting with delight at each touch of lips and tongue on buttery flesh.

And all the time he talked to her, in a low, intimate voice that was another charge on her drunken senses. "You lay in the sun, Anna, the sweat breaking out on your skin, on your thighs, till I could think of nothing but my tongue licking it off, till I could taste the salt of you actually in my mouth...and you knew it and I knew you knew it."

"No," she whispered.

"How I wanted to punish you for tempting me. I dreamed of how I would do this, how I would make you weep with desire and wanting. How my hands and mouth would touch you, caress you, stroke you...my hands on your damp skin, stroking your feet, your thighs, your stomach, your breasts. Sometimes, when you lay on your back, it was like death, the wanting to walk over to you, to put my hand on the fabric of your suit and draw it aside and kiss you there.

"I told myself my tongue would torment

you till you wept for the thrust of my body, and then I would refuse, so that you should know what torment was mine.

"But I knew I was a fool. If once I had touched you, I would have lost all. If I made you beg, at the first pleading I would have to thrust into you. I could not have resisted then."

"Gazi," was all she could whisper.

"Yes, I dreamed of you saying my name in this way," he said roughly, as if the sound of her voice was too much, and held another delicate morsel up to her lips. "And you will say it again for me, in every way that I dreamed."

He looked down at her body, at the bare, soft brown shoulders, the slender curved arms, the soft folds of the fine velvet that covered her breasts. Her nipples pressed against the delicate velvet cloth, announcing her sexual arousal.

She was constantly half fainting. Her blood ran between head and body with a wild rushing that drowned her. She saw him looking down at her body, saw his eyes darken.

He offered her another buttery bite. Looking

into his stormy, hungry eyes, she thought of how she would kiss his flesh, too, and gently took what he offered onto her tongue, half smiling at him in sensuous promise.

The breath hissed between his teeth. "You drive me to the edge," he said in a voice like gravel.

When the meal was over, Anna could scarcely stand. She staggered, her knees turned to butter, and was sure she must look drunk, if anyone were watching them, but she didn't want to find out. Gazi took the coat from the attendant and held it for her, and she could feel his arms like iron with the effort it took not to pull her into his embrace as she slipped her arms inside the sleeves.

Neither of them even noticed the photographers' cameras as they went, hand in hand, his grip so possessive it hurt her, out to the waiting car.

His control lasted until the limousine door shut them in. With a steady hand he pressed a switch, and a blind hummed up to cover the glass between the passenger compartment and the driver's. Another switch plunged them into darkness. Music was already softly playing. Outside the black-tinted windows, the city lights began to slide past.

He reached for her, passion tearing at them both, and with a cry she was in his arms. He drew her across his lap, her head in one possessive hand, his other arm wrapping her waist under the velvet coat, and lifted her up to his mouth for the wildest, hungriest kiss either of them had ever experienced. They were pierced with passionate sweetness, and moaned their pent-up need against each other's lips.

Never had a kiss sent so much pleasure through her body, so that she trembled and clung, shivering with desire. Never had his mouth been so hungry for a woman, so that no matter how he drank, he could not get enough of her. Her arms wrapped his head, her fingers threaded the dark curls, while her mouth opened to his wild demands.

The car stopped, a door slammed, and at last, heaving with breath, they broke apart. She lay looking up at him, seeing nothing but the glint of light on his curling hair; he stared blindly down at her. Like two animals, scenting each other in the darkness.

"We are at the hotel," he murmured.

Her hand was clenched in his hair and Anna had to command her fingers to let him go. She felt the hard, uncomfortable pressure from his groin against her side and smiled as he helped her to sit up.

"All right?" he asked, and she heard the click as he unlocked the door. The chauffeur opened it, and a moment later they were inside the hotel and stepping into the luxurious, golden-lighted elevator that carried them upwards.

In the darkened sitting room, two lamps cast soft pools of light, and a fire had been lit in the grate. They moved towards it without speaking. Beside the fireplace a small table held a decanter and glasses.

"Will you have a brandy?" Gazi asked as he helped her out of her velvet coat. The silky lining brushing her skin was almost more than she could bear. She nodded mutely as he tossed the coat onto a sofa, and he turned to the table.

He lifted the stopper out of the decanter and set it down with a small sound that seemed to resonate around them. The slight gurgling of the liquid, even, was another branch laid on the erotic fire.

He handed her the goblet, the brandy a glowing, rich, warm amber in the bottom. Picking up his own, he swirled, drank, and set the glass down again. Then he bent and hungrily kissed her.

The taste of brandy hit all her senses as he kissed it into her mouth, onto her tongue. Anna felt shivers of sensation from her brain to her toes, and with her free hand clutched at his jacket front, her head going back to allow him the fullest access to her mouth.

His hands enclosed her, one arm around her waist, one hard on her naked shoulder. He lifted his mouth from her mouth, and moved hungrily down the line of her throat. The taste of brandy on her tongue smoked through her system, and hot on its trail little flames of sensation licked their way.

His hand found the little velvet buttons at her back, and one by one began to undo them. Her eyes closed dreamily, the better to follow the progress of his determined fingers down her spine, from between her shoulder blades, down and down along her spine to her waist, while her skin became ever more sensitive.

The buttons stopped below her waist, leaving the whole long stretch of her back naked and accessible to his teasing, tasting hands, and he stroked and caressed the bare skin while his mouth sought hers again.

The room was warm. All her shivers arose in his touch, a curious heated chill running crazily all over and through her. She buried her hand in the thick curls on his head and obediently bent backwards as he pressed her body tight against him.

Her glass was slipping from her grasp, and as he straightened he took it from her and set it down. Then he stood close, looking down at her. The straps of her dress had loosened and were slipping off her shoulders, and she instinctively bent her elbows up, placing her hands against her throat.

"Let it fall," Gazi commanded softly, and his voice, too, was all erotic sensation, compelling her obedience. She dropped her arms to her sides, and the velvet whispered slowly, slowly down over her breasts, leaving them naked to the touch of the fireglow.

He closed his eyes, opened them again, and that, too, created sensation in her. The dress rested precariously on her hips for a moment, clung there, and then, as if reluctantly, slithered down the gentle curve and fell with a little swoop to her feet.

She stood revealed in tiny black briefs, smoky lace-top stockings, delicate high-heel mules, and the diamond circlets at throat and wrist.

His hands reached out to slide with possessive heat down her back and encircle her rump, and he drew her against him, gazing into her eyes with a hotter, brighter flame than the fire provided.

"You will drive me out of my mind," he growled, and as her head fell helplessly back he pressed his lips against the pulse at the base of her throat. Her hands wrapped his neck, slid down his back onto the silky fabric of his jacket.

"Take this off," she murmured, as her hands moved to his chest and slipped inside and against his shirt, pushing the jacket down his arms. He shrugged out of it and let it fall, and now she flirtatiously pulled at his neat black bow tie, untied it, and with a hungry, teasing smile, slowly pulled it away.

He smiled, his eyes dark, and let her work on the tiny buttons, one by one, of his shirt. His chest was darkly warm in the firelight, and as she pulled the shirt down his arms, she laid a line of kisses in the neat curling mat of hair, up and across his shoulder to his throat.

"You have not taken off my cuff links," Gazi murmured protestingly, as his mouth smothered hers in a kiss so hungry she moaned.

Anna smiled. "You're at my mercy, then," she whispered, drawing the shirt further down his arms to pinion him.

He smiled a smile, and lifted his arms, the muscles bulging for a moment of exertion, and then she heard the sound of tearing fabric and the distant clink of buttons hitting somewhere, and his arms were free, each wrist carrying a tattered half shirt. He stopped a moment to tear himself free, tossing the remnants of the shirt wildly away. Then his arms wrapped her tight, dragging her against him with a ruthlessness that told her she had released a demon in him, and swung her up to carry her to his bedroom.

"A little further, Beloved, before we rest."

"Ah, how weary I am with riding! How far to India now, my Lion?"

He looked over his shoulder at the cloud in the distance. "Not far, my princess. Courage."

But her eyes followed his, and now she, too, saw the signs of pursuit. "Riders!" she cried. "Oh, Lion, is it my father?"

"A caravan," he lied. "On its way, like us, to India. We shall join them."

She spurred her mount to a gallop again, and bit her cheek not to cry out against the pain and weariness. They rode in silence, as those behind grew steadily closer.

"Will they catch us, Lion?" she asked.
He did not answer.

Anna awoke from the dream just before dawn, still in his arms. Rain drove against the windows and she lay listening to the music of it.

Never in her life had she been held with such passion as she had felt in Gazi's hands, never had she experienced such a wild storm of pleasure and need as had swept her in his embrace.

When he entered her, it was all fresh, all new, for the joy she experienced had touched a part of her that no one had ever touched in her. Everything that had gone before was like a sepia photograph in comparison. She had clung to him, accepting the thrust of his body from the depths of her self, weeping as pleasure suffused her.

She loved him. She looked into his face now, the faint glow of dawn showing her the mark on his eye, and a passion of tenderness overwhelmed her. Her heart melted in its own burning, and was reborn stronger, surer, understanding things that until yesterday she had only dimly glimpsed.

Of course he did not love her. He was attracted, but for a man like him sexual passion was more a part of his being than her effect on him. She had no illusions about ordinary Anna Lamb's ability to touch his heart.

It would break her heart when her time with him was over. Maybe it would have been better for her if she had resisted the temptation of his lovemaking...but Anna had the feeling that, however much this affair cost her in the end, when she was an old woman she would look back on her moments with Sheikh Gazi as something she was glad to have experienced.

She felt chilly suddenly, and instinctively slipped closer to him. Still asleep, he reached for her, and drew her in against his warm, naked body as if that was where she belonged.

The Sunday papers were delivered to the suite, and as they sat over their breakfast at a table set cozily in front of a bright fire, Gazi and Anna glanced through them.

The story of their arrival in London was not extensively reported, though it had got a few mentions in gossip columns. Only one paper ran a picture on the front page. It was a shot of her looking up at him, and she thought the look between them should set the paper on fire.

Gazi glanced from the paper to her with a look that made her heart jump with sadness, though she couldn't have said why. Perhaps because her pictured face was that of a woman deep in love, and that troubled him.

He shook his head over the favourite story, a rehashed royal scandal. "We must do better than this," he said matter-of-factly, tossing the last tabloid aside and picking up his coffee. "Yusuf cannot be counted on to read gossip columns."

Anna gazed at him. "Do better, how?"

"First things first," Gazi said, with a smile that stopped her heart. "I must take you shopping."

Anna had only ever dreamed of the kind of shopping trip that followed. He seemed to want to buy her everything he saw. She protested several times that he was buying too much, but he simply ignored her.

''Never has so much been purchased by so few in so short a time,'' she joked, as he signalled his approval to yet another outfit, one only suitable for a yacht cruise. At last he said, in a bored voice, ''Anna, you must have clothes if we are going to carry this off.''

''But where will I ever wear these?''

''On my yacht,'' he said with surprise.

''But, Gazi—'' she began again, and he made an impatient sound.

''Anna,'' he told her in a low voice. ''I ask you to remember that you are the pampered darling of a rich Arab, and the mother of his only child. Please, Anna! Cannot you find it in you to be capricious, difficult to please, even a little greedy? You should be saying, 'Can't I have both, darling?' not 'Gazi, you are spending too much on me!' You are doing me a great favour, much more than you know, and it is only right that I should reward you according to my means. Do you think a few thousands spent on clothes means anything to me?''

Then she gave herself up to it—total, guilt-free shopping.

''Can I buy one for Lisbet?'' she asked, when he encouraged her to buy several fashionable pashminas in a variety of colours. Gazi shrugged his approval. ''Buy her a dozen, Anna,'' he said.

His cellphone rang several times as they shopped, and he had brief discussions with the callers. When they had finished their shopping at one famous store, Anna was surprised to hear Gazi say that they would take everything with them.

The store produced several uniformed footmen to carry their packages. Gazi chose a medium-sized shopping bag and handed it to Anna. ''Carry this, Anna,'' he said, and took two small boxes under his own arm.

Followed by the footmen, whose arms were full, he led the way to the exit. Outside they were met by two or three photographers, who snapped their cameras as the little procession, the image of conspicuous consumerism or remnant of a vanished era, depending on your point of view, walked along the pavement to the limousine waiting a few yards away.

When they got into the car, she grinned at Gazi. "You're really good at this!" she said.

"It is a part of my job to be good at it. In any case, it is not difficult to manipulate something like the media," he said. "Greed is the biggest weakness anyone has, whether an institution or an individual."

She eyed him. "Do you think it's right to manipulate people?"

"Anna, if I said to the editors of those papers, 'In the hope of saving my sister's life I need you to run a certain story,' do you think they would agree?"

She thought. "I don't know. Wouldn't they?"

"It is possible. But it is also possible that one of them at least would consider the fact that I am afraid for my sister's life at her own husband's hands a much better story. I do not wish to see a headline tomorrow reading *Save My Sister, Pleads Arab Playboy*."

She was silenced.

They returned to the hotel, where they had

a few hours to prepare for a black-tie function in the evening. Anna had the full treatment again, massage, manicure and pedicure, and professional makeup job.

By the time she was ready for the party she was feeling utterly pampered, and she knew she had never looked better in her life. Her hairstyle wasn't violently different from her old one, but it was a thousand times better cut. Little locks of hair tumbled this way and that over her scalp and down the back of her neck in charming confusion, with half a dozen sapphire-and-diamond trinkets nestling artistically among them, which seemed to reveal a dark sensitivity in her sapphire eyes. Her individual looks and fine bone structure had been dramatized with subtle shading and black eyeliner, and her wide, expressive mouth was coloured dark maroon.

She wore an ankle-length coat dress with a stand-up shirt collar, bodice snugly fitted to the waist, and slightly flaring skirt that was open at the front to well above the knee. It was made of soft-flowing midnight-blue and creamy tan silk brocade that matched both her skin and the deep blue of her eyes. It gave the impression that she was naked under a covering of lace. For warmth she carried one of her new cashmere pashminas, in matching midnight-blue.

She was all blue, black and tan. With clear nail varnish on her short artist's nails, and stockings that matched the navy of the dress, the only flash of real colour was her wine-dark lips. Anna looked dramatic and sensational and, staring at herself in the mirror, she thought that, although she would never be a beauty, perhaps tonight it was just a little less unbelievable that she might be the consort of a man like Sheikh Gazi al Hamzeh.

He was looking extremely rich and handsome himself, in a black dinner jacket with diamond cuff links and diamond button studs nestling among the intricate pleats of an impeccable white silk shirt.

He lifted his head from the contemplation of the fire as she entered the room, and his eyes found her in the huge slanted mirror just above the mantel. His glance darkened in a way that sent blood rushing to her brain, and for a moment neither moved.

Formal wear seemed to emphasize the patch around his eye. He really was a swashbuckler tonight. Anna shivered with a frisson of pure sexual excitement.

"Hi," she said, lifting a hand to shoulder height and waggling her fingers at him, a crazy grin splitting her face.

He turned. "Hi," he returned, smiling with one corner of his mouth, his eyes still intent. "You are very lovely tonight, Anna."

"Amazing what money can do, isn't it?" she quipped, to hide from both of them what admiration in his voice could do to her heart.

"Money can do many things, Anna, but it cannot invent beauty like yours in a woman."

His tone was not consciously caressing, but there was a timbre to his voice that always drew a reaction from her, and coupled with a comment like this, it made her mouth soften tremulously. She couldn't think of anything to say.

"Come and see if you like these," he commanded softly, and opened another jeweller's box to reveal a breathtaking spangle of diamonds and sapphires to match those in her hair. She chose a large square-cut sapphire ring and diamond teardrop earrings, and waved her hands airily.

"I could get used to this!" she joked.

He was watching her with a smile that turned her insides to mush. "Good," he said.

Fifteen

It was a party at a very exclusive private address, with a long line of limos waiting in the sweep drive to disgorge celebrities, and several photographers snapping continually. Anna realized just how exclusive it was, though, only as they moved through the rooms, sparkling with glowing chandeliers, brilliant conversation and an array of jewels on nearly every inch of bare skin. She recognized numerous faces—from film, from television, and even one or two from *Parliamentary Question Time.*

"Gazi, how fabulous of you to come!" a glamorous redhead exclaimed exuberantly.

She was covered head to toe with glittering gold and had an accent Anna couldn't quite place. "And this is Anna! Hellooo!" she crooned, grabbing Anna's hands and kissing her on both cheeks.

"Hello," Anna returned, unable to place her.

"Gazi says that you paint wonderful murals of Moorish palaces that he can't tell from the real thing," the woman said, her eyes searching the crowd for a waiter and summoning him over to offer a tray of champagne. "I hope you will paint something for me. You must come to see me, Anna, and I will show you my small dining room and you will tell me if you can do something Greek with it."

As Anna expressed her enthusiastic willingness, a photographer ambled over. "Can I get one of all three of you?" he called, and the redhead struck a pose, smiling a practised smile. Anna tried to do the same, wishing she had asked Lisbet for a few pointers.

"Of course, we want the publicity," the hostess murmured to Anna. "The editor has

given us a two-page photo spread in the weekend magazine.''

''Thank you, Princess,'' the photographer
said, moving away again.

''My God, that was, that was Princess…
Princess…'' Anna muttered in a low voice,
groping for the name of one of the uncrowned
heads of Europe, as they moved on a few
minutes later. Gazi smiled down at her.

''She is the patroness of the charity,'' he
said.

''Charity?'' Anna repeated, and then threw
a glance around the glittering assembly. ''Is
this a *charity* function?''

Her sense of humour was sparked, and she
flicked a look up into his face, trying to sup-
press a smile, an effort that only added to the
charm of her expression. As she met the ap-
preciative glow in his own eyes she bit her lip
and her head went back, and a crack of delighted laughter burst from her throat, causing
a few heads near them to turn.

''Sheikh al Hamzeh, my dear chap! What a
very great pleasure!'' a white-haired man cried
in the crusty tones of the Establishment, and a

moment later they had been absorbed into the group and Anna was talking to a famous television host.

The evening that followed was one she thought she would always remember. Gazi was blandly informing everyone who asked—and everyone did—that they had met when he bought a painted screen from her to put in his Barakat home.

So Anna was asked for her business card by several people who said they were in the middle of redecorating or about to redecorate and would love to have her do something, and also by the television host, who seemed to have a more personal interest in mind. That boosted her sexual confidence amazingly, because Gazi gave the man a look that would have quick-frozen strawberries in June.

Then she reminded herself that he was here to manipulate people into believing he cared. She must be careful not to fall for the act herself.

But the whole evening was made delicious by his constant attendance, the possessive brush of his hand over her back, the look of sometimes lazy, sometimes urgent desire in his eyes. She knew it was only partly true, but then it was only partly false. And it was headier than the champagne.

They stayed till after midnight. Then, as they left the party, she discovered just how much Sheikh Gazi al Hamzeh was a master of media manipulation.

''The first editions have now gone to bed,'' he explained quietly as they moved to the door. ''They now would like something new for the later editions. Will you play along with me, Anna?''

''All right,'' she said nervously. ''What are we going to do?''

''We are going to have a spat and make up,'' he murmured.

The temperature had dropped while they were inside, and when they emerged on the pavement the waiting photographers were huddled under the awning, looking miserable and stamping their feet against the cold. Most of them only eyed the couple. They had pictures of them going in, and there was nothing to be gained by another identical shot of them coming out.

Gazi paused to tip the doorman. ''Don't be stupid!'' he murmured over his shoulder to her in low-voiced masculine irritation, as if continuing an argument begun inside.

The lights showed a driving wet snow coming down at an angle, and although the doorman had clearly been busy with the broom on the red carpet that covered the pavement under the awning, snow was settling again.

''Why is it stupid?'' Anna muttered furiously. Her blood was singing with mingled nerves and excitement. He looked so handsome and powerful in his navy cashmere coat, his white silk scarf over the black bow tie, mock anger flashing in his eyes. ''It's not stupid!'' She turned away from him towards the curb.

''Anna!'' he commanded, striding after her, and reaching a hand to clasp her arm. Anna whirled and snatched her arm away.

''I don't appreciate being called stupid!''

The gusting wind suddenly cooperated. It whipped the split skirt of her dress out behind her, revealing all the length of her slim legs, thighs bare above her lace-top stay-ups, and incidentally freezing her where she stood. The photographers, who had slowly been waking up, now snapped to attention.

As she whirled, Anna accidentally put her foot straight onto a little mound of cold slush. She slipped, half gasped, half screamed, and instinctively clutched at Gazi. A second later she felt her feet go entirely out from under her as electric warmth embraced her. Gazi was scooping her up in his arms.

''Excellent, Anna!'' he murmured in her ear, and she felt the heat of him rush through her chilled blood.

He had his arm under her bare knees. As he lifted her, the skirt fell away, revealing her legs right up to the hip. Her shoes dangled from her toes. The photographers were scrambling now, calling encouragement and approval, as Anna, freezing, futilely groped for the panels of her skirt.

''Don't cover your legs! You will soon be warm,'' Gazi whispered in her ear in a firm command that was suddenly charged with an erotic nuance, and set her heart racing. "Look at me, Anna, and relent!"

Her breath catching in her throat, she lifted one arm to his shoulder and glanced uncertainly into his face. He paused for a few moments, smiling down at her with sexy promise, as if his imagination, too, had suddenly moved into high gear. Cameras clicked and flashed all around them, and then Gazi stepped to the limousine that was just purring up the drive, and after a moment she was inside.

Instantly she was locked in his arms, being ruthlessly kissed. His hand slid up her stockinged thigh with a touch like cold fire, because his flesh was chilled but still heated her blood.

Haunting music played, the windows were all covered, and recessed light glowed softly, enclosing them in their own little world. Anna was half sprawled on the luxurious leather under him, her legs angled, her dress up around her hips, revealing everything as Gazi lifted his mouth, straightened and gazed at her. But as she made a move to sit, he pushed her back with one hand, while the other unerringly found its way to the lace at the top of her stockings, traced its way over the bare skin above, and then, with ruthless precision, to a spot behind the lace of her bikini panties.

Anna gasped. She found she could make no move, no protest, to prevent what he intended. Sensation shot through her, as much from the look in his eyes as from his touch, as he carefully stroked and stroked the potent little cluster of hungry nerves.

They responded obediently to his dictates, as if instantly recognizing their master. A breathless little grunt escaped her, and her hips moved hungrily. She saw the corner of his mouth go up, and one strong arm was on her thigh then, lifting her leg over his head as he sat, and resting it on his other side—spreading her wide for his eyes, his hands...his mouth.

She understood his intent as he bent forward. His hand stopped its delicate stroking and instead his fingers slipped under the lace of her briefs and pulled it to one side, and then, just as he had promised, his mouth was against her, his tongue hot, teasing, hungry.

Her hands clenched in his hair. She could do nothing, say nothing. She was completely at his mercy, melted into submission by the shafts of pure, keening pleasure that his mouth created in her.

"Gazi!" she cried, hitting the peak with a suddenness that made her heart thump crazily. Honeyed sweetness poured through her as her back arched and her muscles clenched.

"Another," he urged her in soft command, and she felt how expertly his fingers toyed with her and his tongue rasped her to pleasure again. She felt completely open, completely helpless, as if the pleasure he gave her put her in his power. "Again," he said, and like an animal going through a hoop, her body had to obey.

After an endless time in a world of pleasure, she found him relenting. He restored her clothing, and drew her body up so that she sat in his embrace, her back against his chest, his face in her hair.

"What's happening?" she begged, hardly knowing where she was.

"We are almost at the airport," he murmured, and she could still shiver as his voice whispered against her ear.

"Oh!" she exclaimed. She had completely forgotten that tonight he had said they would fly back to West Barakat. She lifted a bare foot. "My shoe's gone," she said stupidly.

He felt behind him and eventually found it, and Anna marvelled that she had the muscle coordination necessary to slip it onto her foot. Then the limousine rolled to a stop and it was only moments before they were back on the private jet again, very like the first time, except that this time, Gazi was looking at her with a promise in his eyes that tonight she would not spend the hours in that bed alone.

They weren't long in the air when the hostess approached them with a small tray of Turkish delight and a low-voiced query. Gazi turned to Anna. "Would you like a nightcap or a hot drink, Anna? Or do you prefer to go straight to bed?"

She did not like being offered a choice. She wanted him to want to take her to bed as much as she wanted to go. So perversely, she said, "Oh, let's have some coffee."

She bit into a deliciously soft sugary cube

and then stared absently at the shiny green inside of the half still between her fingers.

"Of course," he said, and she couldn't read his expression. "How much sugar?"

"Sweet, please."

He spoke to the hostess, who smiled, nodded, and disappeared into the galley.

Meanwhile Anna unbuckled her seat belt and settled more comfortably in the big plush armchair. With a little whisper of silk, her dress slithered away to reveal all the length of one leg, encased in the dark cobweb of expensive stocking he had bought for her.

Gazi's gaze was instinctively drawn, then moved up to her face, with a look that abruptly reminded her of what had taken place in the limousine. The heat of the memory invaded her body, burned her cheeks.

As the hostess set a little cup of thick sweet liquid in front of her, Gazi reached for a powdery cube of Turkish delight and put it in his mouth with a lazy hand. Anna felt electricity in the air, felt her eyes forced up to his face. He tilted his head and met her gaze, and Anna's heart kicked as if it wanted to kill her.

"I am glad you do not want to sleep," he said.

She yearned towards him, body and soul; she was almost weeping with love and desire. She said, half meaning it, "I don't intend to waste a moment of my allotted time, Gazi."

His eyes darkened with dramatic suddenness, and only then did she realize with what an iron hold he was controlling himself. He reached to imprison her hand, took the little cup from her fingers with his other, and set it down.

"Then let us not waste a moment," he told her through his teeth, and a moment later he had pulled her to her feet and was leading her to the stateroom.

The bed with its snowy linens was inviting, the room luxuriously intimate, with the ever-present hum of the engines seeming to cut them off from the world.

She melted into passionate hunger as he unbuttoned her dress and drew it off her shoulders, and kissed him with little hungry bites as she in turn unbuttoned his shirt, his trousers, and stripped everything except his underwear off. Then at last, with desperate hungry kissing, they fell onto the bed and their hands began a passionate roaming over each other's body.

He stroked her silken legs, stripped the fine lace from her breasts, while her hungry hand found his sex and pressed it in demand.

Their blood raced up, too needy to wait, and when he stripped off the last of the lace that hid her from him, and tore off the cloth from his own hips, she cried little cries of encouragement and need, and spread her legs, her body ready for the hard, hungry thrust of his.

It was as much pleasure as he could bear, thrusting so suddenly into her, and he drew out and thrust again, to see the grimace of pleasure on her face. Neither of them knew how long they went on, crying out their pleasure, until desire and love and sensation exploded into a fireball of sweetness that burned new pathways all through their being.

They bathed their faces at the little spring, and then turned towards the dust cloud that

told them how close their pursuers approached.

"It is not a caravan, Lion," she said sadly.
"It is my father."

"It must be so, Beloved."

"They will kill us," she said. "I am sorry
for one thing only," and he marvelled at her
bravery, for her voice held no quiver, no
doubt.

"What, then, Beloved, do you have regrets?
I for myself have none," he said.

"Only one, my Lion. That we had nor time
nor place to taste each other's love before we
die."

"Ah, that," he said.

"Give me your small sword," she commanded. "For my life will cost them almost as
dear as yours."

He pulled the little blade from his belt. "Beloved, do you indeed wish it so?"

"What, shall I die a coward's death at my
lover's hands? How would we face each other
in the other world, if I asked this of you?"

His heart wept to see her so stalwart.

"One day," she said. "One day, we shall

meet. Somewhere, somehow. Do not you feel it?''

He was silent.

''It is so!'' she swore. ''If we but wish it! Swear to me that it shall be so!''

The Lion drew his sword and laid his hand upon the blade. ''As God is my witness, though we die here, I will wander a lost soul until your words are fulfilled, Beloved.''

''So be it,'' she said. ''And when we have found each other, then we will live all the life we lose now. For God rewards true lovers for their constancy. How can He do else?''

Sixteen

It was early afternoon at the villa, and they were sitting over a late lunch on the terrace by the pool when the call came through.

Nadia was alive. Jaf had already been to see her. Gazi told her that much before embarking on a long conversation with his brother, while Anna sat waiting in anxious impatience for the details.

"She jumped off the bridge," he told her when at last he put the phone down. "The water level in the Thames was high that night. That saved her."

Anna bit her lip and tried to find the right things to say. He took her hand and kissed it.

"Someone in one of the moored houseboats saw her go. They rescued her. She begged them not to go to the police, told them if her husband found her he would kill her. The man was a surgeon. He admitted her to a private hospital. Since then she has been too ill to say anything. When she recovered a little, she phoned the only number she could remember. Fortunately it was the number of our apartment in London and Jaf was there."

He sat in silence, contemplating it, until she prompted him. "What about Ramiz?"

A shadow crossed his face. "The reason she felt hopeless enough to jump was—when Ramiz discovered she was pregnant, he promised to return here to West Barakat and ask us to begin divorce proceedings on her behalf. She never heard from him again.

"Yusuf must have suspected something, for suddenly she was a prisoner in her own home. She knew nothing of Ramiz's disappearance, but she knew that if Ramiz had spoken to me she would have heard. She thought Ramiz had proved faithless. Yusuf became more and more jealous, till she was frightened for her life and her child's. You were right, Anna. She went into labour and saw it as her only chance. She fled, and gave birth in a garage.

"Only then did she understand she had nowhere to flee to. We were not in town, and our apartment is the first place Yusuf would look for her. After months of bravery, Nadia broke. She caught a cab, left the baby in the cab without letting the driver know, walked onto the bridge and jumped."

They were silent, trying to understand her despair.

"And I got into the cab," Anna murmured at last.

"Yes, Nadia said a woman was there as she got out. She said she looked at you, silently entrusting her baby to you."

Anna shook her head. "I still don't have any memory of it. She must be very relieved to know that you have Safiyah safe."

"Yes, of course. She regrets very deeply what she tried to do, and we will bring her home here as soon as possible to be with her baby.''

''But you're still worried,'' Anna said. ''Is it something about Ramiz?''

Gazi looked at her, weighing his words, and the look in his eyes made her sad with fear. ''Yes, partly about Ramiz. It concerns more than Nadia, or Safiyah, or Ramiz. It is personal, but also much more than personal. It may involve the national security of the Barakat Emirates.''

Her breath came in on a long, audible intake.

''If I tell you, Anna, it will put a burden of secrecy on you. You can never mention it to anyone, not even your friend Lisbet. Can you accept this? Will you hear me?''

''Are you working for Prince Karim?''

''I am his Cup Companion. Of course I work for him. In this matter, for all the princes.''

''Are you a spy?''

''It is not my usual job. But we all do whatever is necessary.''

Anna gazed out over the terrace to the blue

sea and wondered how it was possible for a life to change so dramatically in such a short time. How had it happened that she was sitting here in this fabulous villa, whose existence she had known nothing about two weeks ago, being invited to hear the state secrets of the Barakat Emirates?

"If you tell me all this, you're then going to ask me to do something?"

He swallowed, and her heart clenched nervously. "Yes, I will ask you something. But I want to tell you, not to persuade you to anything, but because I am tired of secrecy between us."

Her heart began to thud. "From the beginning I have been forced always into a position of suspecting you against my natural inclinations, Anna. I could not do or say the things I wished, because so much more than my personal happiness or even my sister's life was at stake. If I was indeed blinded to your true self, the whole country might suffer. Now I ask your permission to tell you the truth."

Anna swallowed against the lump of fear

and nerves that choked her. "Yes," she said. "Please tell me."

"You know already that Ramiz was on an undercover assignment for the princes. What I did not tell you was that his mission was to infiltrate, if possible, a secret group trying to overthrow the monarchy here."

Anna silently opened her mouth. She could hardly breathe.

"We think that it was not by his own design that Ramiz met Nadia again. We have suspected that his investigations led him to Yusuf. What Nadia says seems to confirm this."

"Oh, my God! You mean Yusuf is part of the conspiracy?"

"Yusuf must not have known that Nadia was in love before her marriage. My father kept her secret. If he had known, it is impossible to believe that he would have brought Ramiz home to meet his wife, as she says he did. But Ramiz—Ramiz knew who Yusuf was. Pity Ramiz, whose mission required that he accept the invitation!"

"How dreadful!" she breathed, and bit her lip, feeling how totally inadequate that was.

"Do you now understand, Anna, why I was forced to lie to you and abduct you and accuse you? It is not merely the princes' lives that are at risk from this conspiracy. A move to overthrow their rule would bring certain civil war to Barakat. Tribe against tribe, brother against brother. It would bring to the surface many rivalries now in abeyance. The repercussions would last beyond this generation, whatever the outcome. Our personal lives were less important than this.

"Can you accept that I thought and acted in this way, Anna?"

She nodded, her head bent, not daring to hope for what might be coming next. "To have you here, to be falling more and more under your spell with every moment that passed, to understand how faulty my own judgement might be...to have to suspect that you did this to me deliberately...to be forced to lie—I hope you did not suffer so much at my hands that you cannot also pity me, Anna."

Still she could not lift her head.

"Look at me," he commanded in a firm,

quiet, lover's voice, and her heart kicked protestingly and then rushed into a wild rhythm
as she looked at him.

"I love you, Anna. When you are here, this
house, the house of my ancestors, is complete
for me. Wherever I am, when you are there,
too, I am home. Stay with me. I don't ask you
to give up your art. Anna, I live more than half
my time in Europe—we can work it out.

"You already love me a little, I think. You
would not look at me with such eyes when I
make love with you, if you did not love me a
little. Is it not so?"

She bit her lip and gazed at him. "Oh,
Gazi!" she whispered.

"Let me finish," he pleaded. "I see you
with my sister's child and I know that you are
the mother I want for my own children. I know
that somehow, you got in that taxi that night
because we had to meet, you and I. And we
did meet.

"Don't make me let you go. Marry me, and
I will make your love grow. If ever a man
could make a woman love him, Anna, I know
that I can make you love me."

His urgency impelled him to his feet, and he drew her up into his arms. They stood in the nook formed by the ancient arch, against a trellis spread with flowers and thick greenery, his strong arms protectively around her. A delicate perfume drifted down as their bodies made the flowers tremble.

"Gazi," was all she could say, but that word told him everything.

*   *   *   *   *

LARGE PRINT TITLES FOR
JULY - DECEMBER 2004

SILHOUETTE®
SPECIAL EDITION™

July:	THE BABY LEGACY	Pamela Toth
August:	THE BRIDE SAID, 'SURPRISE!'	Cathy Gillen Thacker
September:	WHO'S THAT BABY?	Diana Whitney
October:	THE VIRGIN BRIDE SAID, 'WOW!'	Cathy Gillen Thacker
November:	A MAN ALONE	Lindsay McKenna
December:	MILLIONAIRE'S INSTANT BABY	Allison Leigh

SILHOUETTE®
DESIRE™

July:	THE LAST SANTINI VIRGIN	Maureen Child
August:	SHEIKH'S WOMAN	Alexandra Sellers
September:	THE PREGNANT VIRGIN	Anne Eames
October:	RANCHER'S PROPOSITION	Anne Marie Winston
November:	TALL, DARK AND WESTERN	Anne Marie Winston
December:	HER BABY'S FATHER	Katherine Garbera

SILHOUETTE®
SENSATION™

July:	THE WILDES OF WYOMING—ACE	Ruth Langan
August:	THE UNDERCOVER BRIDE	Kylie Brant
September:	EGAN CASSIDY'S KID	Beverly Barton
October:	ROGUE'S REFORM	Marilyn Pappano
November:	NIGHT OF NO RETURN	Eileen Wilks
December:	NEVER BEEN KISSED	Linda Turner

0704-1204 Silh LP